MW00637146

ADVENTURE TIME

The Official Cookbook

The Official Cookbook

Monster-Fighting Meals, Dungeon-Crawl Desserts, and Princess-Worthy Pancakes from the Land of Ooo

RECIPES BY **JORDAN GROSSER**

TEXT BY **CHRISTOPHER HASTINGS**

PHOTOGRAPHS BY **ANDRIA LO**

INSIGHT ☉ EDITIONS

San Rafael, California

THE
FOUNDERS' ISLAND KITCHEN

VALUABLE MEALS FOR HEALTHY FAMILIES

FIRST EDITION

OUTSIDE ADDITIONS PUBLISHING

CONTENTS

GREETINGS TO MOTHERS, FATHERS, ambitious children, bachelors, and spinsters. We caretakers of culinary knowledge welcome you in your quest for nutritious, delicious meals prepared in the home. We, the authors at Founders' Island Kitchen, believe deeply in the value of

New Introduction BY ME, FINN

WHAT IS UP?! Wait, no. You don't have to answer that. I know you are reading a book. Anyway, hey, I am Finn . . . of the past! I discovered this book on Founders' Island, and I honestly feel gronked up in my emotion zone about it. Jake's always talking about food as an expression of love (and his nachos prove it), so having a cookbook as a connection to humans—my mom especially—geez. Even if it's weird and old, this is a big deal to me.

I've flipped through the book and noticed that a lot of the pages are missing. I figured that I, Finn, should take on the quest of adding awesome-sauce recipes to these pages. I mean, why have a regular hamburger when you and your stomach can take on a Hamburger Monster! And Finn Cakes are something that should be preserved for all of time forever, of course.

After that, I still had a bunch of blank pages on my hands, so I asked all of my chef-y Ooo friends to help out, too!

We've got a breakfast section that's mostly empty? So what? I know a whole *kingdom* of Breakfast People! Precious ink in the appetizers section has been washed away by the cruel tides of time? Well, my bro Jake still remembers how to make his nachos, and that's all the appetizer you need. Sides? Mains? Desserts? Again, I can literally walk a couple miles and find a kingdom of people dedicated to each of these food groups.

So check it out and eat it up! We have old recipes we've done our best to re-create, as well as cool Ooo recipes that probably should have been written down a long time ago anyway!

BREAKFAST

WHETHER IT IS A WORKING WEEK DAY or a relaxing weekend, a breakfast must be included in the diet. A hearty and filling meal at the start of the day is just the thing to keep the spouse happy, the children quiet, or the crippling loneliness at bay. In this section you'll find plenty of recipes sure to provide the energy you and your f~~amil~~...

This vaguely creepy cookbook is right! Breakfast is pretty important! In fact, I can see Breakfast Princess eyeballing this book right now, probably trying to rip out all the other sections. That's how important it is. Aah! She's coming this way! She's got a crepe spear! —Jake

BACON PANCAKES
11

SAUSAGE BREAKFAST PARTY PIZZA
13

YEEARGH! ON TOAST
14

BANANA GUARD BANANA BREAD
15

CINNAMON BUN
17

FRENCH TOAST DIP SANDWICH
19

It is the sovereign right of the Breakfast Kingdom to write all breakfast-related texts and treatises, and so I have confiscated this book and . . . very well. The dog is yelling about breakfast right now, and it appears he has the appropriate reverence. We shall appoint him an official Ambassador of Breakfast and allow him to include his bacon pancake recipe in this most noble section.

Onward, to breakfast! —Breakfast Princess

Bacon Pancakes

By Jake

This book had what looked like a pancake recipe, but I ripped it out and tore that page up. Why? Because a plain old pancake has no place in Jake's kitchen. Pancakes require creativity and upgrades, like bacon!

What could make hot fluffy pancakes better than hickory-smoked goodness? It surprises me that we don't come out of the womb with, like, ancestral knowledge that pancakes deserve bacon the same way they deserve syrup and butter. But I guess that's what cookbooks are for. Did I mention this was a good idea, Finn?

Pancakes

2 cups all-purpose flour

3 tablespoons sugar

1 ½ teaspoons baking powder

1 teaspoon baking soda

¼ teaspoon salt

4 eggs

2 cups buttermilk

½ cup butter, melted

⅓ pound smoked bacon, cooked crisp and diced

Walnut Butter

1 cup walnuts, soaked for 24 hours then drained

1 ½ teaspoons walnut oil or canola oil

1 tablespoon honey

1 tablespoon butter

A pinch of salt

Maple Jelly

¾ cup maple syrup

3 ounces cold water

1 cup apricot jelly

FOR THE PANCAKES

1. Combine dry ingredients (flour, sugar, baking powder, baking soda, salt) in a large mixing bowl.
2. In a separate bowl, whisk together wet ingredients (eggs, buttermilk, melted butter), then slowly add the dry ingredients until mixed thoroughly.
3. Heat nonstick pan over medium heat and coat with nonstick spray. Using a serving spoon, carefully place a large spoonful of batter on pan, allowing the batter to fall straight off the tip of the spoon and naturally form an even circle.
4. Cook until bottom side is nicely browned, then sprinkle the crisped bacon generously onto the pancake and flip immediately to cook the other side and seal the bacon into the pancake. Continue with the remainder of the batter.
5. Dress the pancakes with as much walnut butter and maple jelly as you'd like, and serve immediately.

FOR THE WALNUT BUTTER

1. Preheat oven to 350°F and place walnuts on baking sheet in a single layer. Toast in oven for 12 to 15 minutes.
2. Once the walnuts have cooled, place them in a food processor and process until they have reached the consistency of a paste.
3. Slowly add the rest of the ingredients until mixed thoroughly. You may need to scrape the sides of the food processor throughout the process in order to make sure the walnut butter is combined well.

FOR THE MAPLE JELLY

Combine all the ingredients in a blender or food processor and blend at high speed until thoroughly combined. Place in a container, cover, and chill for at least two hours before using. This will allow the jelly to firm up a bit.

Sausage Breakfast Party Pizza

Makes: 8 slices

BY PARTY GOD

PIZZZZAAAAAA!!! YES! IF TO PARTY IS TO LIVE, THEN TO EAT PIZZA IS TO BREATHE! BUT WHAT HAPPENS IF YOU PARTY TOO FAR INTO THE MORNING TO EAT NORMAL DELICIOUS LUNCH OR DINNER PIZZA?

EASY! YOU ADD SOME EGGS AND BREAKFAST MEATS ON THE PIZZA AND THEN PIZZA-PARTY YOUR WAY THROUGH THE MORNING! A BREAKFAST PIZZA MAKES YOU MASTER OF THE DAY! YOU REFUSE THE RULES! YOU EAT PIZZA FOR BREAKFAST! YOU'RE SO COOOOOL! AAARROOOOOOOOOOOO!

3 ½ cups bread flour

1 teaspoon sugar

1 package active dry yeast

2 teaspoons salt

1 ½ cups warm water (110°F)

1 teaspoon chopped rosemary

½ teaspoon chopped sage

2 tablespoons + 2 teaspoons olive oil

½ cup pizza sauce

1 cup mozzarella

6 ounces breakfast sausage, sliced

1 green onion, chopped

2 eggs

1. Combine flour, sugar, yeast, and salt in a stand mixer bowl. Connect dough hook attachment to the mixer.

2. While the machine is on slow speed, add water, rosemary, sage, and 2 tablespoons of olive oil.

3. Adjust mixer to a medium speed and allow dough to form a ball and pull away from the sides of the mixing bowl, for 3 to 4 minutes.

4. Cover the mixing bowl with plastic wrap and place to rest in a warm spot, allowing dough to double in size.

5. Turn the dough out onto a lightly floured surface. Divide it into two equal pieces and roll into a ball shape. Cover each with a kitchen towel or plastic wrap and let them rest for 10 minutes before rolling out the pizza dough.

6. Preheat oven to 450°F.

7. Gently pound out the dough into a round disc, and roll out until you have a 10- to 12-inch round. Transfer to a round pizza pan or greased baking sheet.

8. Spread on pizza sauce and sprinkle cheese, sausage, and green onion on top.

9. Crack two large eggs on each half of pizza dough.

10. Place in oven for 10 to 12 minutes, until bottom of pizza is crisp but not burnt.

Yeeargh! on Toast

By Ice King

What's this? A cookbook? Why wasn't I invited to share my frozen anchovies recipe?! Well, if that's the way Finn wants to be, then I'll just have him try a cold jar of Yeeargh! After he tries this savory, delicious spread, he'll be begging me to write the whole book.

½ cup black sesame paste

¼ cup soy sauce

1 tablespoon onion powder

3 tablespoons nutritional yeast

1. Place all ingredients in a blender and puree ingredients, starting slowly and working your way up to high speed. Add water a teaspoon at a time if necessary in order to thin the mixture out enough so that the ingredients move freely in blender.

2. Spread mixture on toast, sandwiches, crackers, etc.

OKAY!, SO I TRIED MAKING THIS RECIPE. IT TURNS OUT THAT "YEEARGH!" IS THE NOISE I MADE UPON SOILING MY TASTE PALACE (AKA MOUTH) WITH THIS GOO! THIS IS NOT FOR EVERY PALATE, DUDES. —FINN

BANANA GUARD
BANANA BREAD

Sometimes you just cannot eat all the bananas that you purchased from the local grocer. Sometimes you like to watch those bananas turn as black as the darkest parts of your soul. This delightful bread recipe provides an alternative for very ripe bananas. Happy baking!

MAKES: 1 loaf

1 ¾ cups all-purpose flour	½ cup unsalted butter
1 teaspoon baking soda	½ cup sugar
½ teaspoon salt	½ cup light brown sugar
½ teaspoon ground cinnamon	¼ teaspoon vanilla extract
3 ripe bananas	2 large eggs
1 teaspoon lemon juice	¼ cup buttermilk

¼ CUP CHOCOLATE CHIPS

YAY, BANANA BREAD! THIS OLD RECIPE NEEDS CHOCOLATE. I LIKE CHOCOLATE. —BANANA GUARD

1. Preheat oven to 350°F. Sift together flour, baking soda, salt, and cinnamon in a large bowl. In a separate bowl, mix bananas and lemon juice into a lumpy but soft mixture.
   AND CHOCOLATE CHIPS

2. Beat butter, sugar, brown sugar, and vanilla at low speed for 1 minute or until combined. Increase speed to medium and beat 1 ½ to 2 minutes, until light and fluffy. Add eggs one at a time, beating until blended after each addition.

3. Add flour mixture to butter mixture alternately with buttermilk, beginning and ending with flour mixture. Add banana-chocolate chip mixture, beating just until batter is blended. Pour batter into a well-buttered and floured 8- x 4-inch loaf pan and place on a baking sheet.

4. Bake at 350°F for 55 to 60 minutes. Cool in pan on a wire rack for 10 minutes. Remove the bread from the pan and transfer it back onto the wire rack. Let cool for 50 minutes.

I just picked up this book after Cinnamon Bun dropped it and ran away screaming. Reader, he gets confused easily. Don't worry. We take care of him. —Flame Princess

Cinnamon Bun
By Cinnamon Bun

"Cinnamon Bun." Hey! This must be my diary! I don't remember writing it, but I guess that's why you keep a diary in the first place! You forget stuff.

Hmm, I definitely don't remember "dissolving yeast in warm water," but I guess it's just something I did one day! And then decided to write down! Ha ha, just Cinnamon Bun things, I guess?

Wait, I went in an oven? When did I go in an oven?! And I got out?! This diary is revealing some dark secrets about my past!

Dough

3 tablespoons unsalted butter

1 cup whole milk

3 ½ cups unbleached all-purpose flour

½ cup sugar

1 large egg

2 ¼ teaspoons rapid-rise yeast

1 teaspoon salt

Nonstick vegetable oil spray

Filling

¾ cup golden brown sugar

2 tablespoons ground cinnamon

¼ cup unsalted butter, room temperature

Glaze

4 ounces cream cheese, room temperature

1 cup powdered sugar

¼ cup unsalted butter, room temperature

½ teaspoon vanilla extract

FOR THE DOUGH

1. Melt butter into milk in a saucepan on the stove until melted and warm, not boiling hot. Pour into bowl of stand mixer fitted with paddle attachment. Add 1 cup flour (hold on to the rest), sugar, egg, yeast, and salt. Beat on low speed for 3 minutes, stopping occasionally to scrape sides of bowl. Add remaining 2 ½ cups flour. Beat on low until flour is absorbed and dough is sticky. If dough is very sticky, add in more flour by the tablespoon until dough begins to form a ball and pulls away from sides of bowl.

2. Turn dough out onto lightly floured work surface. Knead until smooth and elastic, adding more flour if sticky, about 8 minutes. Form into ball.

3. Lightly oil large bowl with nonstick spray. Transfer dough to bowl. Cover bowl with plastic wrap, then kitchen towel. Let dough rise in warm, draft-free area until doubled in volume, about 2 hours.

FOR THE FILLING

1. Mix brown sugar and cinnamon in medium bowl.

2. Punch down dough. Transfer to floured work surface. Roll out to 15- x 11-inch rectangle. Spread butter over dough. Sprinkle cinnamon-sugar mixture evenly over butter. Starting at one long side, roll dough into log, pinching gently to keep it rolled up. With the seam side down, cut dough crosswise with thin, sharp knife into 18 equal pieces. They should look like pinwheels.

3. Spray two 9-inch square glass baking dishes with nonstick spray. Divide rolls between baking dishes, arranging the cut side up. There will be almost no space between rolls.

4. Cover baking dishes with plastic wrap, then kitchen towel. Let dough rise in warm, draft-free area until nearly doubled in volume.

5. Position rack in center of oven and preheat to 375°F. Bake rolls until tops are golden, about 20 minutes. Remove from oven and invert immediately onto rack. Cool 10 minutes. Turn rolls right-side up.

FOR THE GLAZE

Combine cream cheese, powdered sugar, butter, and vanilla in a medium bowl. Using electric mixer, beat until smooth. Spread glaze on rolls.

French Toast Dip Sandwich

Makes: 4 sandwiches

By Breakfast Princess

Ah! Some blank space that allows for commentary from the Breakfast Kingdom itself. As the Breakfast Princess, it is my duty to continue to inform the world of breakfast's status as the most important meal of the day. We in the Breakfast Kingdom treat the meal as a sacred ritual. Several courses. Countless plates.

This Breakfast Sandwich was created during the Brunch War. It gave soldiers the strength to carry on and win the border between lunch and breakfast (which is 11:00 a.m.). Eat it in their honor. Wash your hands afterward. They'll be sticky.

French Toast

4 large eggs

1 tablespoon sugar

1 cup milk

¼ teaspoon salt

8 slices Texas toast

1 tablespoon butter

Sandwich Filling

8 slices bacon, cooked

4 fried eggs

4 slices cheddar cheese

1 cup maple syrup

FOR THE FRENCH TOAST

1. Preheat oven to 350°F. Break eggs into a medium mixing bowl. Add sugar, milk, and salt and whisk lightly.

2. Prepare a large skillet on medium heat with a bit of the butter to coat the pan.

3. Place bread slices in egg mixture one at a time, allowing each to soak up moisture for a few seconds. The bread needs to go directly from the egg mixture to the hot pan, so only soak as many slices at a time as the pan will fit.

4. Sear each slice in the pan until golden brown on both sides. Continue until all the bread is soaked and seared.

FOR ASSEMBLY

1. Assemble sandwich with a piece of French toast topped with two slices of bacon, a fried egg, and a slice of cheddar, closed off with another piece of French toast.

2. Place the whole sandwich in the oven until cheese is melted. Serve with a side of maple syrup.

APPETIZERS

WHEN HOSTING COMPANY, nothing puts the thought of restaurant dining superiority out of the minds of guests like a good, small portion to stoke the appetite. If hubby's boss makes an unexpected appearance just before dinner or the wife's charitable turn leads her to invite a hobo over to tea, you're going to want these recipes at your fingertips to

YOU KNOW WHAT I LIKE ABOUT SNACKS? IT MEANS I GET TO EAT WHENEVER I WANT TO OUTSIDE OF OPPRESSIVE BREAKFAST, LUNCH, AND DINNER TIMES. ALSO, I GET TO EAT THOSE TIMES, TOO. ALSO, I HAVE DISCOVERED THAT SNACKS ARE PROBABLY THE MOST FUN FOODS. SNACKS ARE LIKE, "HEY, FRIEND, DINNER'S NOT WATCHING. WHY NOT EAT WHAT YOU REALLY WANT? *CHEESE ON EVERYTHING.*"
—FINN

Ultimate Cheesy Nachos
23

The Most Elegant Ambrosia Salad
25

Spoons of Prosperity Soup
26

Deviled Eggs
27

Flame Kingdom Wings
29

Chili of the Nightosphere
31

Snacks! Yeah, snacks! —Jake

Ultimate Cheesy Nachos
By Jake

All right, so one time Lady and I went to Tablecloth and Too Many Cups: A Food Experience. It's the fanciest restaurant, and we wanted a special evening out.

When the waiter came to take our order, I let him know my problem! There were no nachos on the menu! "Nachos?!" he scoffed. "Nachos are college trash food. Cheese on a chip. You jest, dog! You jest!"

Well, no. No, I don't. Nachos are an ideal expression of contrast and harmony in food form! Anyway, ten minutes later the waiter and I were both shouting, and then Lady and I got kicked out of the restaurant. Enjoy the nachos.

Two cheeses, baby!

One 14-ounce package tortilla chips

½ cup cheddar cheese powder

8 ounces shredded chicken

¼ cup small-diced onion

1 teaspoon finely chopped jalapeño

½ cup small-diced avocado

½ cup shredded mozzarella

½ cup shredded cheddar

¼ cup chopped cilantro

Only if you like it! Finn says it tastes like soap. —Jake

1. Preheat oven to 400°F.

2. Place tortilla chips on a cookie tray or casserole dish large enough to hold them and put in oven for 90 seconds. Immediately toss chips in a bowl with the cheddar cheese powder, coating the chips thoroughly. Think about snooty restaurants that refuse to do this simple step.

3. Arrange chips on a large, oven-safe platter or casserole dish, spreading the chips out as evenly as possible.

4. Spread chicken, onion, jalapeño, and avocado evenly over chips, and finish with the two cheeses to cover all the other ingredients. Hold on to that cilantro for when the chips come out of the oven.

5. Put platter in the oven for 8 to 12 minutes, making sure the cheese is evenly melted.

6. Finish by topping with cilantro (unless you're one of those people who thinks cilantro tastes like soap and grass) and serve next to a bowl of your favorite salsas and hot sauces.

Hey! Hey! Put beans on it! Put beans in the nachos! I cook mine on a campfire, but I guess if you're, like, the president of money, and you have a stove or microwave, you can heat them up that way, too. —Lumpy Space Princess

This is just a little recipe that I've been working on. Don't you dare judge it! —Ice King

The Most Elegant Ambrosia Salad

By his royal majesty,
Prince Gumball

Dearest, dearest reader,
I am a prince who is burdened but also blessed with a rich, thriving kingdom. Hundreds of citizens fill my streets and bang on my door. To be a prince of such a demanding nation, one has to be ready to host richly, simply, and quickly! When a throng of fifty or more Chocolate Boys demands a diplomatic banquet with the endless Peanut Butter Babies, the host prince has to be ready to treat them elegantly at a moment's notice! Enter the Ambrosia Salad! Exotic fruits and sweet cream seem a salad only gods may taste. Truthfully, it's as easy as dumping any mix of junk together. Yum!

1 cup whipping cream

2 tablespoons sugar

1 teaspoon vanilla extract

¾ cup shredded toasted coconut

1 cup yogurt

1 cup raspberries

1 cup blackberries

2 cups strawberries, quartered

½ cup blueberries

1. In a mixing bowl, whisk together cream, sugar, and vanilla until you have stiff peaks of whipped cream.

2. Gently fold in coconut and yogurt using a rubber spatula, until all ingredients are combined. It's important to fold the ingredients together gently to keep the mixture as light and airy as possible.

3. Finish by folding in the fruit and letting the mixture sit in the refrigerator for about 2 hours, covered tightly, before serving.

4. This can be topped with some fresh mint and basil or some cinnamon and a ginger cookie. Don't add mint if you are hosting Mint People. Don't add basil if you are hosting Basil People, etc.

Spoon of Prosperity Soup

BY FINN

It's probably worth jotting down how the Spoon of Prosperity works. Balance it on your nose and be rejuvenated! Just like eating the normal way! If y'all's don't have a Spoon of Prosperity, you can substitute in a normal spoon. You should probably substitute something to eat with the spoon, too. Actually, just forget the whole actual Spoon of Prosperity. When we went to find it, we got trapped in a sand dungeon, and our friend Marceline went crazy hungry, and I found out I was color-blind! Not the best day.

2 tablespoons olive oil

1 cup small-diced onion

½ cup small-diced carrot

1 tablespoon chopped garlic

1 ½ cups peeled and
   seeded diced tomato

2 quarts beef stock

1 ½ cups cooked white beans

1 cup thinly chopped Swiss chard

1 cup cooked farro or quinoa

¼ cup grated Parmesan cheese

1. In a heavy bottomed saucepot, sauté the onions, carrot, and garlic in the olive oil on medium heat until onions are soft.

2. Add tomato and beef stock and simmer for about 45 minutes on medium-low heat. The heat should be just enough to keep a little movement on the surface of the soup, but it should never come to a full boil.

3. Add the white beans and chard to the pot and simmer for about 10 minutes. Add the farro or quinoa just before serving.

4. Finish each bowl by topping the soup with the grated Parmesan.

Nice, dude!
Cheese my soup
all day long.
— Jake

So I'm paging through this book and I see this page on how to boil an egg, and I'm like, "Whoa, whoa, hey, not a lot of *DEVIL* going on here, if you catch my meaning. Let's get this egg *DEMONED UP* the way it should be." Boil the eggs in the fires of the Nightosphere and follow the recipe, which I totally promise will not steal your soul or promise me your firstborn.
-- Hunson Abadeer

DEVILED EGGS By Hunson Abadeer

What evening of gentlemanly card games, sporting competitions, or picture shows would be complete without this delicacy? See page ~~11~~ for the proper way to use and duel with egg spoons.

MAKES: 12 servings

6 eggs, hard-boiled and peeled

¼ cup mayonnaise

1 teaspoon yellow mustard

½ teaspoon dill relish

½ teaspoon sweet relish

Pinch of salt

Pinch of ground black pepper

Smoked Spanish paprika, for garnish

Cut each egg in half lengthwise and carefully separate the yolks into a small mixing bowl. Add the mayonnaise, mustard, relishes, salt, and pepper. Mash together with a fork until you have a smooth consistency. Place a large, heaping spoonful of the yolk filling back into the empty egg white halves, sprinkle lightly with paprika, and they are ready to serve.

SUGGESTED ADDITIONS

• Smoked salmon, capers, dill

• Barbecue pulled pork, bread-and-butter pickles

• Potato chips, sliced prosciutto, chives

• Chilled asparagus, Parmesan, lemon zest

Nightosphere Additions
• Bones, any kind.
• Red-skinned eggs from devil birds.
• Nightosphere dirt spice.
• A shameful whisper.

27

Flame Kingdom Wings

by Flame Princess

Wings of a chicken fried and basted in sauce hot enough to dissolve a human tongue? We know this dish! Hot wings! They're like little edible batteries for Flame People! Since the original recipe was clearly missing the necessary Scoville units for keeping a Flame Person healthy, I made some alterations. Serve to a Flame Person friend or human enemy.

1 ½ pounds of chicken wings

2 tablespoons vegetable oil

1 tablespoon garlic

½ cup red barbecue sauce

¼ cup pomegranate juice

¼ cup honey

1 tablespoon salt

2 tablespoons sugar

1 teaspoon cayenne (5 tablespoons for a Flame Person)

2 teaspoons fennel seed powder

½ teaspoon star anise

1 teaspoon coriander

4 teaspoons cumin

½ teaspoon cloves

64 fluid ounces peanut oil

1. Preheat oven to 300°F.

2. Cut the wings at the joints, discarding the tips. Put wings in a mixing bowl and coat with half of the vegetable oil. Season with salt and pepper.

3. Place on a baking tray in the oven and cook completely through, for 25 to 35 minutes.

4. Allow them to cool off for about 15 minutes and place in freezer until frozen solid. This takes about 8 to 10 hours. This process results in a crispier chicken wing.

5. Place the rest of the vegetable oil and garlic in a saucepan on medium heat and stir until softened. Then add barbecue sauce, pomegranate juice, honey, salt, sugar, cayenne, fennel seed powder, star anise, coriander, cumin, and cloves.

6. Bring the ingredients to a boil for about 1 minute, stirring constantly, and then remove from heat and set aside. If not using immediately, keep refrigerated and gently reheat before using.

7. In a 6-quart pot, bring the peanut oil up to 350°F, using a candy thermometer to measure temperature. Gently place about eight chicken wings in the pot at a time, frying until the wings are crispy and golden in color.

8. Toss the wings in the sauce in a mixing bowl, coating them thoroughly.

OH MY GLOB, I DID THIS TO IMPRESS HER, AND I HAD TO GO TO THE HOSPITAL. STICK TO ONE TEASPOON. —FINN

Chili of the Nightosphere

Makes: 6 servings

By Hunson Abadeer

Oh, an ancient human cookbook! How quaint! I remember the humans! Wild bunch, those ones.

And I'll tell you, they never got wilder than they did with their chili. I won't get into the issue of Texas-style vs. rest-of-the-world-style. But I *will* tell you that what makes a fine chili is the, uh . . . well, it's the chilies.

Down in the Nightosphere, most of us have been undead for a *really* long time, so it takes some *serious* spice in our bowls to wake us up. I traveled far across the varied ghost worlds and finally found *ghost chilies*, just the thing to kick up a bowl so a dead man can taste it.

If you're alive, adjust to taste.

1 tablespoon vegetable oil

1 pound onion, small-diced

1 tablespoon minced garlic

1 ½ pounds ground 80/20 beef

⅓ cup dark chili powder

1 tablespoon achiote paste

16 ounces cooked kidney beans

12 fluid ounces chili sauce

2 tablespoons Worcestershire sauce

Salt and pepper to taste

Optional: A chopped-up ghost pepper if you're waking the dead.

1. In a heavy-bottomed saucepan, sauté the onion and garlic in the vegetable oil over high heat until lightly caramelized.

2. Add ground beef to the onions and brown until beef is about medium-rare. Do not stir the beef around too much. You want delicious large clumps of beef in the finished chili, not gritty-bitty beef.

3. Immediately add chili powder, achiote paste, kidney beans, chili sauce, and Worcestershire sauce to the pot.

4. Cook on medium heat, stirring gently on occasion until chili is hot and beef has finished cooking through. Serve immediately while it's nice and hot. You know not to just leave chili around to get cold after you're done cooking it, right? Whatever, who knows who got their hands on this. Eat the chili warm, okay?

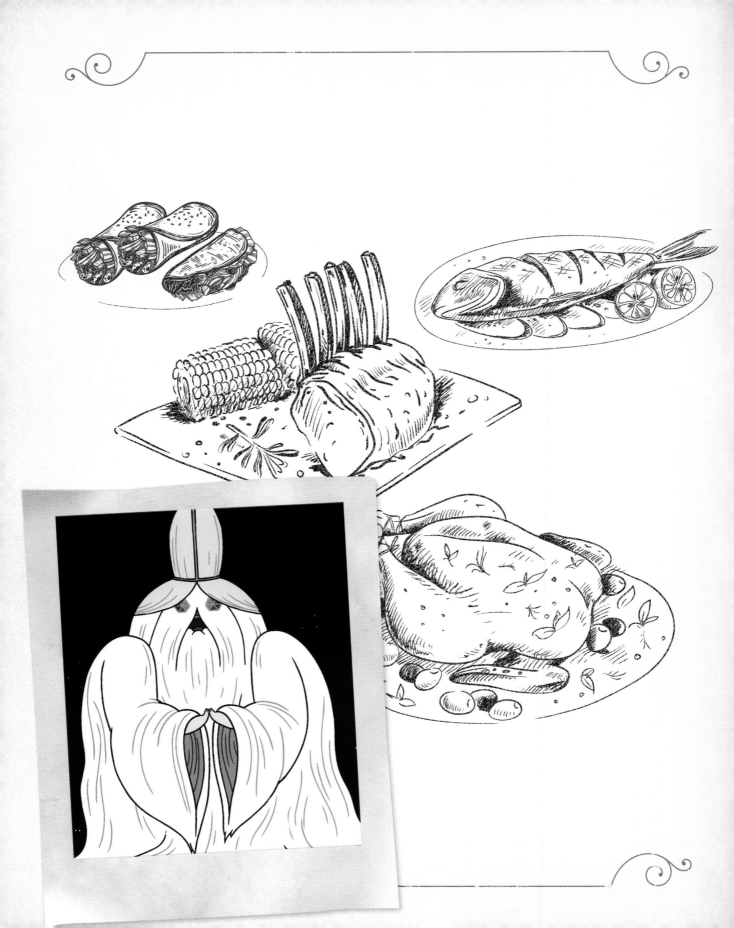

MAIN DISHES

A GOOD PIECE OF FOOD at the heart of one's supper will make the body happy and rich in health. Here are recipes for any occasion, including but not limited to lawn bowling tournaments, ~~selecinado i~~...

SO YEAH, I LOVE A NICE MEAL AT A NICE TIME! THAT'S WHAT A MAIN DISH IS ALL ABOUT! AND IT'S NOT JUST MEAT! WE'VE GOT TASTY FRIED RICE DONE UP SO DEMONS DON'T BUG YOU. JAKE PROMISED HE'LL SHARE HIS PERFECT SANDWICH RECIPE, WHICH IS INSANE. (AND THEN PRINCESS BUBBLEGUM INSISTED SHE PUT IN *HER* PERFECT SANDWICH, WHICH . . . WELL, YOU TRY IT. IT'S A DIFFERENT KIND OF PERFECT, I GUESS.) WE'VE GOT BURGERS AND PASTA (OH BOY, PASTAS), AND JAKE IS ALL ABOUT FIXING THE BURRITO RECIPE WE FOUND. NOW LET US PARTAKE OF . . . THE MAINS. —FINN

Jake's Most Delicious Sandwich

BY JAKE
(TRANSCRIBED BY FINN)

Sorry, reader! Sorry, book! Jake started talking about his perfect sandwich and started drooling all over the page. We're in the bathroom now, and he is dictating the recipe to me from the bathtub, which he is safely filling with drool and—hold on.

Dude, we just had to drain the tub of drool. How is there that much liquid in Jake?! Is this recipe safe to share with someone who may not have Jake's magical drool-replenishing abilities? I don't want you to think about this sandwich and start drooling and get dehydrated. That would be very unheroic of me.

It's a crime not to share, though. Here's Jake's perfect sandwich!

4 sourdough baguettes, lightly toasted

Fried Chicken and Lobster

Three 4 to 5 ounces boneless, skinless chicken thighs, quartered (12 pieces)

2 lobster tails, poached and quartered (8 pieces)

1 ½ cups buttermilk

1 teaspoon salt

½ teaspoon dried parsley

½ teaspoon dried thyme

1 tablespoon Dijon mustard

1 teaspoon garlic powder

¼ teaspoon black pepper

Pinch of cayenne

1 quart canola oil

3 cups flour

1 tablespoon salt

Dill Cream Cheese Spread

½ cup cream cheese

¼ cup mayonnaise

1 tablespoon fresh dill, chopped

¼ teaspoon salt

Pinch of black pepper

1 lemon, juiced and zested

FOR THE FRIED CHICKEN AND LOBSTER

1. After quartering the chicken, you will have 12 pieces; after quartering the lobster tails, you will have 8 pieces. Once the chicken and lobster are fried, each sandwich will get 3 pieces of chicken and 2 pieces of lobster.

2. In a mixing bowl, whisk together buttermilk, salt, parsley, thyme, mustard, garlic powder, black pepper, and cayenne. Divide the mixture in two. Marinate chicken in one half and lobster in the other, for at least 8 hours before frying.

3. In a saucepan, bring the canola oil up to 325°F. While the oil is heating up, add flour and salt to a bowl large enough to toss the chicken and lobster. When the oil has reached temperature, coat the chicken and lobster in the flour mixture before placing carefully in the fryer oil. The chicken will take longer, so start with it first. Coat the pieces of chicken one by one, allowing as much of the flour mixture as possible to cover the chicken. It is recommended to cook about half the chicken at a time in two batches. After generously coating each piece of chicken, lightly tap the piece on the side of the bowl, knocking off excess flour before carefully lowering it into the oil.

4. Fry the chicken for 5 to 7 minutes, until it's cooked through. Remove it from the oil using a slotted spoon. Rest meat on a paper towel to soak up excess oil. Continue the process with the rest of the chicken and lobster until you have perfectly crispy, fried, delicious nuggets of joy. Each piece of lobster should take 3 to 4 minutes to cook through.

5. While the last batch of lobster is cooking, lightly toast the bread in the oven.

FOR THE DILL CREAM CHEESE SPREAD

Combine ingredients in a small mixing bowl and mix with rubber spatula until all ingredients are completely incorporated. You may want to use a whisk to finish the process and smooth it out once it's easier to mix.

FOR THE CUCUMBER RELISH

Combine all ingredients in a mixing bowl, toss together, and check for seasoning.

FOR ASSEMBLY

After toasting the baguette, slice it open on one side but not all the way through, so that you have something that resembles a boat to fill with sandwich ingredients. Start by spreading some dill cream cheese on both sides of the baguette. Place three pieces of chicken and two pieces of lobster on each sandwich. Top sandwich with a generous helping of the cucumber relish. Look around to make sure Magic Man is nowhere nearby to steal your sandwich, and eat it in a time bubble that protects him from your intervention. Enjoy!

Cucumber Relish

¼ cup peeled, seeded, and small-diced English cucumber

¼ cup small-diced yellow onion

¼ cup small-diced dill pickle

¼ cup small-diced tomato

2 teaspoons olive oil

¼ teaspoon salt

Pinch of black pepper

Half of a large lemon, juiced

Pinch of red chili flakes

35

Princess Bubblegum's Perfect Sandwich

By Princess Bubblegum

Hey, gang. Chef Peebles Von Goodcook here. (I like to try out different names for different theoretical professions. Being stuck with "Princess Bubblegum" gets tiring sometimes. And the cookbook is fun!)

I know you just read a lot of hype on the soggy pages of what Jake thinks a sandwich should be, but I have a more *scientific* approach. This sandwich may appear humble, but each ingredient is a crucial member of the sandwich team. Miss one, and the sandwich mission fails—and you're eating a sad bunch of dumb junk, crying. Just crying.

2 slices of sourdough bread

½ teaspoon butter

1 tablespoon mayonnaise

1 to 2 leaves of little gem lettuce

2 slices of Gruyere cheese

4 slices of tomato, ¼-inch thick

5 medium-sized basil leaves

Salt and pepper to taste

1. Pop bread in toaster. We can all agree bread is better after going through a nice Maillard reaction!

2. As soon as bread comes out of the toaster, spread both slices with an equal amount of butter and allow to melt into the bread.

3. Spread half the mayonnaise on one piece of bread. Top with the lettuce, cheese, and tomatoes and season with salt and pepper.

4. Top the tomatoes with basil leaves.

5. Spread the rest of the mayonnaise on the last slice of bread, and finish building your sandwich.

Whitewater
HOME-STYLE MAC 'N' CHEESE

Here's a fun tip for the impoverished students in our readership: You can survive off a pot of this mac 'n' cheese for close to a month if you play your cards right. Remember to take a multivitamin before each meal. Founders' Island takes no responsibility for scurvy, rickets, inside-out stomach syndrome

MAKES: 8 servings

4 cups dried macaroni

¼ cup butter

¼ cup flour

2 ½ cups milk

2 heaping teaspoons dry mustard powder

1 pound sharp white Cheddar, fresh grated

Pinch of salt

OPTIONAL INGREDIENTS:

1 cup canned tuna

1 cup frozen peas

> I make this dish all the time, but I prefer it with a few extra additions. I pretend that the noodles are little boats, the tuna is tuna, and the peas are boulders ready to send the little sailors to a cheesy grave. It makes for a very exciting meal.
>
> —Minerva

1. Cook the macaroni until still slightly firm. Drain and set aside.

2. In a large pot, melt the butter and sprinkle in the flour. Whisk together over medium-low heat. Cook for a couple of minutes, whisking constantly. Don't let it burn.

3. Pour in the milk, add the mustard, and whisk until smooth. Cook until very thick, about 5 minutes.

4. Reduce the heat to low and slowly begin adding cheese, melting it into the sauce before adding more cheese.

5. Season with salt and fold in pasta with any other optional ingredients until it is very hot and ready to serve.

OH MY GLOB, DUDES! THIS IS A NOTE FROM MY MOM! AND I TOTALLY EAT MY MAC 'N' CHEESE THIS WAY!!!
—FINN

Magic Barbecue Ribs

BY MAGIC MAN

MAAAGIC! I used my amazing powers to change old train parts into gooey ribs! Just follow this recipe, and you too will have tangy barbecue sauce flowing through you like moonlight through a ghost dance. Everyone is welcome to share these magic ribs: rats, weeds, tiny manticores . . .

4 tablespoons brown sugar

2 tablespoons granulated onion

2 tablespoons granulated garlic

2 tablespoons paprika

2 tablespoons chili powder

2 teaspoons dry mustard

1 tablespoon salt

1 tablespoon black pepper

2 racks of St. Louis–style ribs

3 cups barbecue sauce

1. In a small bowl, mix together the brown sugar, onion, garlic, paprika, chili, mustard, salt, and pepper.
2. Sprinkle the rub on both sides of the slab of ribs and rub it into the meat well.
3. Wrap the ribs in a few layers of aluminum foil and let them sit in the fridge for a couple hours.
4. Preheat oven to 300°F.
5. Place ribs on a baking sheet and put in the oven for 2 hours.
6. Take the ribs out of the foil. Brush some of the barbecue sauce on both sides.
7. Grill them for 4 to 5 minutes on each side or until they start to char and the sauce is bubbling hot.

Sweet and Sassy Meatball Pizza

Makes: 8 slices

By Pizza Sassy's

Everyone should eat more pizza! Pizza Sassy's would *love* the business! But if you don't have a Pizza Sassy's in your neighborhood (which is in the Candy Kingdom and the Candy Kingdom only), you can make my pizza at home.

3 ½ cups bread flour

1 teaspoon sugar

1 package active dry yeast

2 teaspoons salt

1 ½ cups warm water (110°F)

2 tablespoons olive oil

½ cup pizza sauce

1 cup shredded mozzarella

3 meatballs, sliced

1 teaspoon chopped garlic

5 to 6 basil leaves

1. Combine flour, sugar, yeast, and salt in a stand mixer bowl and connect dough hook attachment to the mixer. While the machine is on slow speed, add water and olive oil.

2. Turn mixer to a medium speed and allow dough to form a ball and pull away from the sides of the mixing bowl, for 3 to 4 minutes.

3. Cover the mixing bowl with plastic wrap and place in a warm spot, allowing dough to double in size.

4. Turn the dough out onto a lightly floured surface. Divide it into two equal pieces and roll into a ball shape. Cover each with a kitchen towel or plastic wrap and let them rest for 10 minutes before rolling out the pizza dough.

5. Preheat oven to 450°F.

6. Gently pound out the dough and roll it out into a 10- to 12-inch disk. Transfer to a round pizza pan or a greased baking sheet.

7. Spread the pizza sauce and sprinkle the cheese, meatballs, garlic, and basil onto the pizza dough.

8. Place in the oven for 10 to 12 minutes, until bottom of pizza is crisp but not burnt.

Soy People Tofu

By Lady Rainicorn
(Translated from Rainicorn)

Rainicorns used to love eating humans! They've unfortunately gone largely extinct. Before that happened, my people developed this artificial substitute made from soy. You can't beat tasty soy! Shape it into hands or elbows or whichever part of a human you wish you could eat!

16 ounces silken tofu

6 eggs

2 cups chicken stock

1 tablespoon soy sauce

1 teaspoon sesame seeds

¼ cup green onion, chopped

1. Preheat oven to 300°F.

2. Place the tofu, eggs, chicken stock, soy sauce, and sesame seeds into a blender and puree the ingredients thoroughly at low speed for about 45 seconds. You have now made a custard base.

3. Pour the custard evenly into six 10- to 12-ounce ceramic ramekins or oven-safe cups. (Coffee mugs work great for this.)

4. After you have distributed the custard into each cup, cover the top of each with aluminum foil and place them into a casserole dish in which they can all fit. Fill the casserole dish with hot water halfway up the ramekins or cups.

5. Place in oven for 30 to 45 minutes or until the custards are set and a little jiggly in the center but not loose.

6. Carefully take the casserole dish out of the oven and the ramekins or cups out of the dish. Uncover and garnish each with green onion. Serve immediately.

I MUST ADMIT, IF THIS IS WHAT HUMAN TASTES LIKE . . . I'M DELICIOUS. —FINN

ONE TIME I MET A BUNCH OF FOOD BOYS WHO HAD T-BONE STEAKS FOR HEADS AND WATERMELONS FOR BODIES. IT MADE ME THINK THAT IT MIGHT BE NICE TO TRY HAVING THIS WITH SOME WATERMELON! OR IT MIGHT BE DUMB. THE FOOD BOYS *WERE* KIND OF GULLIBLE AND SINGLE-MINDED. HELPED ME GET OUT OF A WEIRD FANCY GIANT'S LAIR, THOUGH. —FINN

T-BONE STEAK

After a long day at the office, classroom, or tree-themed amusement park, a perfectly cooked steak can mean the difference between a pleasant family meal and a night of cold silences and bitter resentment.

MAKES: 2 servings

One 8-ounce jar of Dijon mustard

1 tablespoon cracked black peppercorns

1 teaspoon chopped garlic

1 teaspoon salt

1 teaspoon chopped thyme

2-pound T-bone steak, about 2 inches thick

¼ cup vegetable oil

1. In a medium bowl, mix the mustard, pepper, garlic, salt, and thyme and then cover the steak completely in the mixture. Wrap tightly with aluminum foil, being careful not to tear the foil. Place in refrigerator overnight. Unwrap the steak and scrape most of the ingredients off of it, but don't be afraid to leave a nice layer of marinade coating it.

2. Preheat oven to 350°F. In a large skillet or cast-iron pan on high heat, add the vegetable oil and, when it starts to smoke, carefully lay the steak in the pan, turning down the heat slightly. Sear each side for about 4 minutes and then place in the oven for about 6 minutes. Allow to rest on a cooling rack for 5 minutes before serving.

OPTIONAL SIDE: COLD, REFRESHING WATERMELON!

WATERMELON CHIMICHURRI

2 CUPS LIGHTLY PACKED CHOPPED PARSLEY

3 TO 5 CLOVES GARLIC, MINCED

1 TEASPOON SALT

1/2 TEASPOON FRESHLY GROUND PEPPER

1/2 TEASPOON CHILI PEPPER FLAKES

1 TABLESPOON FRESH MINT

3 TABLESPOONS FRESH OREGANO LEAVES

3 TABLESPOONS SHALLOT, MINCED

3/4 CUP VEGETABLE OR OLIVE OIL

3 TABLESPOONS SHERRY WINE VINEGAR

3 TABLESPOONS LEMON JUICE

1 CUP DICED WATERMELON

PLACE ALL INGREDIENTS IN A BLENDER OR FOOD PROCESSOR AND PULSE UNTIL WELL CHOPPED BUT NOT PUREED.

WHY WAS EVERYBODY LOOKING AT ME SO NERVOUSLY WHEN THEY GOT TO THIS PART OF THE BOOK? YOU THINK I CARE ABOUT FISH? I DON'T CARE ABOUT FISH. I'M A FLOATIN' BONE LADY WHO CAN MAKE BLUE FLAMES! EAT YOUR FISH STICKS. DON'T YOU WORRY ABOUT OFFENDING GARY THE MERMAID QUEEN.
—GARY THE MERMAID

BAKED SALMON FISH STICKS WITH GREEN DIPPING SAUCE

While an afternoon motoring in the countryside or a weekend safariing on the continent may do wonders for the constitution, nothing beats eating an entire bucketful of fish sticks for fun and profit.

MAKES: 4 servings

1 pound salmon filet, skinned

3 cups panko breadcrumbs

3 eggs

1 tablespoon water

1 tablespoon Old Bay seasoning

WE FOUND AN ENTIRE ABANDONED BOAT FULL OF THIS STUFF! CANS WITH CRABS ON THEM. IF YOU CAN'T FIND AN ABANDONED BOAT FULL OF "OLD BAY," COME BY OUR PLACE AND GET ONE. —FINN

Preheat oven to 450°F. Cut salmon into 1- by 4-inch strips. In a shallow bowl, mix Old Bay seasoning into breadcrumbs. In another bowl, add 1 tablespoon water to the eggs and beat. Dip the fish in the beaten eggs, coating the fish completely, then roll into the breadcrumb mixture, pressing gently to help them stick. Place in a single layer on parchment paper-lined baking sheets. Bake the fish sticks until crisp throughout, for 12 to 15 minutes.

GREEN DIPPING SAUCE

2/3 CUP CHOPPED BELL PEPPER

1/4 CUP SUNFLOWER SEEDS

1 CUP CHOPPED CILANTRO

1/2 CUP CHOPPED PARSLEY

1 TEASPOON CHOPPED JALAPENO, NO SEEDS

1 SLICE OF TOASTED BREAD, NO CRUST

1/2 TEASPOON BLACK PEPPER

3/4 TEASPOON SALT

1/4 TEASPOON CHILI FLAKES

1 LEMON, JUICED

PLACE ALL INGREDIENTS IN A BLENDER. BLEND ON HIGH SPEED UNTIL MIXTURE IS SMOOTH. SEASON TO TASTE.

Anti-Demon Fried Rice

Makes: 2 servings

By Jermaine

So, I used to live in my parents' old house, acting as kind of a caretaker against all the various demons that Dad locked up or cheesed off. A crucial element to this duty was a circle of protection around the house, cast from ancient powerful salts. One night, my brother Jake used a pinch of the salt in some fried rice. I'll admit the salt added a crucial flavor element to the fried rice. Buuuuut it also allowed some demons through the barrier and ended with the house burned to ash and me livin' on the road for a while.

But here's where I discovered something *else* about the salt! If you eat it, it keeps demons from possessing you! This is probably why demonic possessions are actually a pretty rare occurrence. People get a reasonable amount of salt in their diet. So fry up some of this rice and tell a demon to go stink in a hole for awhile!

2 tablespoons peanut or vegetable oil

¼ cup diced Chinese lap cheong sausage

¼ cup diced shiitake mushroom

¼ cup diced raw shrimp

½ teaspoon garlic, grated

½ teaspoon ginger, grated

2 cups long grain rice, cooked and chilled

¼ cup green onion

¼ cup green peas

1 teaspoon soy sauce

¼ teaspoon sugar

¼ teaspoon white pepper

¼ teaspoon sesame oil

Salt to taste

Seriously, I've been skipping this for years like a fool. Put that salt in. — Jermaine

1. In a large sauté pan (nonstick would be helpful), heat the peanut oil on high until the oil is hot. All of these ingredients should be cooked on high, emulating the high-heat, quick-cooking process of a wok. It can be tricky, but after a couple tries, you'll get the feel for it.

2. Carefully toss the sausage and shiitake mushroom in the pan and begin moving the ingredients around, making sure to cook evenly.

3. Add shrimp, garlic, and ginger and continue to cook on high, moving the ingredients around and making sure to evenly cook them.

4. When the shrimp are about halfway cooked through, add the rice, then the green onions and green peas, making sure you don't have clumps in the rice. The more loose and separated the rice is, the better it will come out.

5. Once the rice has been cooking for 2 to 3 minutes—again, moving it around so all the rice gets fried evenly—add the soy sauce, sugar, white pepper, sesame oil, and salt.

6. Mix the fried rice well to incorporate the seasoning thoroughly, cooking the soy sauce into the rice for about 30 seconds. Serve immediately.

Everything Burrito By Jake

Man, when you make a burrito, you gotta *make a burrito*. Stick everything you got in there. I've taken the liberty of adding a few of my extra favorite burrito ingredient suggestions as well (until I ran out of room), but there's really only one crucial ingredient: *the biggest tortilla you can find.* Get a tortilla of legend, buddy. Get a tortilla you thought could only exist in myth. Get a tortilla you could use as a tent. Then wrap up every delicious food you can find in it, like a fat swaddled baby!

Carne Asada

One ½-pound skirt steak

1 cup orange juice

¼ cup lime juice

1 tablespoon finely chopped garlic

½ teaspoon smoked paprika

2 teaspoons cumin

½ teaspoon black pepper

¼ teaspoon ground cloves

Pickled Onion

1 cup slices of red onion, ⅛-inch thick

1 cup water

1 cup red wine vinegar

½ cup sugar

1 tablespoon salt

1 teaspoon pickling spice

Burrito

2 cups tater tots, cooked crispy

Four 14–inch flour tortillas

2 avocados

½ cup chopped cilantro

½ jalapeño, sliced very thin

1 cup shredded cheddar cheese

1 cup crumbled Cotija cheese

½ cup sour cream

FOR THE CARNE ASADA

1. Cut the skirt steak into two large pieces.
2. Combine all ingredients in a container that will hold everything and marinate the steak for 24 hours.
3. The best way to cook this is on the grill, but a saucepan will do the trick. Cook on high heat, searing the meat well on both sides.
4. Turn the heat down a bit until steak is cooked to medium all the way through.

FOR THE PICKLED ONION

1. Put the red onions in a container large enough to hold all the ingredients.
2. In a medium saucepan, bring water, vinegar, sugar, salt, and pickling spice to a boil.
3. Pour over the red onions. Make sure the onions stay submerged and allow them to sit for at least 24 hours before refrigerating.

FOR ASSEMBLY

1. The trick here is to have all of the hot ingredients make it into the burrito while they are still hot. Start by preheating the oven to 425°F. Put the tater tots in the oven for about 25 minutes. Save one of the oven racks to heat the tortillas up really well before you wrap each burrito up.
2. Cook the steak, being sure to let it rest for at least 5 to 8 minutes before slicing it up to put in the burritos.
3. Once the meat is cut up, immediately put the first tortilla in the oven. Take it out once hot, along with the finished tater tots.
4. Start building your Everything Burrito. Add meat and tater tots, followed by pickled onions, avocado, cilantro, jalapeño, cheddar cheese, Cotija cheese, and sour cream. Be sure to split up the ingredients evenly among the burritos.
5. You could also put in various lettuces, kimchi, raw eggs, scrambled eggs, eggs florentine, fried chicken, chicken adobo, boneless chicken wings, French fries, cucumbers, ground beef, salted preserved hams, spicy sauces, salsa verde, old newspaper, filet of cod . . .

Hamburger Monster

BY FINN

Makes: 1 burger monster

One time, me and Jake were goofin' around makin' hamburger sandwiches, just, like, noticing you could keep adding ground beef and make a bigger and bigger hamburger! But then the Life Giving Magus came by. And he accidentally touched the burger. That gave the burger horrible, unnatural life, and it went on a totally bonkers rampage. I had to slay that burger! I didn't feel great about it. That burger was our monster son! But it had to be put down. Once it was slain, it still tasted great. Here's how to make it! Don't add magic! The magic didn't really add any flavor. Just hassle.

½ pound 80/20 ground beef

1 teaspoon Dijon mustard

1 tablespoon smashed roasted garlic

1 teaspoon sweet relish

¼ teaspoon salt

¼ teaspoon black pepper

2 slices white sharp cheddar cheese

1 sesame-seed Kaiser roll

4 to 5 slices of Multiverse Pickles (page 64)

Ketchup, to taste

1. Mix the beef, mustard, garlic, sweet relish, salt, and pepper in a bowl until the mixture is well combined.
2. Shape the meat into a burger patty about ¾ inch to 1 inch thick.
3. This can be cooked either in a pan or over a grill at medium-high heat. You want to sear both sides for about 4 minutes a piece.
4. About halfway through cooking the second side, place the slices of cheese on the hamburger patty so they melt while the burger finishes cooking.
5. Remove the patty from heat and set aside, allowing to rest for 2 minutes.
6. While the hamburger is resting, place the bun either in the pan or on the grill to toast for about a minute.
7. Place the burger on the Kaiser roll and top it with pickle slices and ketchup to your liking.

Uh, hey, Prisma here, popping in from the future of this book. I have a great pickle recipe in here, and you would be a fool not to combine those pickles with this burger. Okay, that's it. See you in the Sides section on page 64.

–Prisma

49

SPAGHETTI AND MEATBALLS

When your snobby neighbor Mr. Wensleydale calls your décor shabby and your doily collection trite, then you can make this spaghetti and smile to yourself because your meatballs are *fancy*. They have three kinds of meat and an actual egg in them. Take that, Mr. Wensleydale!

MAKES: 12 servings

MEATBALLS

2 pounds ground veal

1 pound ground pork

1 pound ground beef

1 cup fresh breadcrumbs

2 tablespoons chopped parsley

½ cup grated Parmesan cheese

2 teaspoons kosher salt

½ teaspoon black pepper

1 extra large egg, beaten

½ cup ice water

SAUCE

1 tablespoon olive oil

1 cup small-diced onion

1 ½ teaspoons minced garlic

One 28-ounce can plum tomatoes

1 tablespoon chopped parsley

1 ½ teaspoons salt

½ teaspoon black pepper

PASTA

One 1-pound package
  of spaghetti

1. Preheat oven to 325°F. For the meatballs, combine the veal, pork, beef, breadcrumbs, parsley, Parmesan cheese, salt, pepper, egg, and water until everything is mixed thoroughly. Roll into desired size and then place on a greased baking sheet. Bake for 20 minutes.

2. To make the sauce, heat olive oil on medium-high heat. Add onions and garlic and sauté until soft, but do not caramelize. Add tomatoes, parsley, salt, and pepper. Allow to come to a boil and immediately turn the heat down to medium-low. Simmer for at least an hour, stirring occasionally. Once the sauce is well seasoned and tasting good, add the meatballs to simmer in the sauce. Bring a pot of water to a boil to cook the spaghetti.

3. Once the pasta is cooked and strained, cover with the sauce and serve topped with the meatballs.

Hot Dog Monster

By Jake

When Finn was just a little boom-boom baby, he was *terrified* of roving Hot Dog Monsters, so our dear mama made these tiny hot dogs that Finn could eat and conquer!

She'd put out a bowl of Softy Cheese and say, "Quickly! Destroy the Hot Dog Monsters before they attack!" And then Finn would dip them in the cheese and eat them.

He defeated the Hot Dog Monster in the dungeon just fine, but, one day Finn judo-tossed one right into a bubbling pit of lava! Just like Mama taught! But Mama didn't teach Finn that Hot Dog Monsters could scream. . . .

Finn eats fewer hot dogs now.

One 10-ounce package refrigerated biscuit dough

4 hot dogs

4 slices pepper jack cheese

Ketchup, to taste

Mustard, to taste

1. Preheat oven to 400°F.

2. Open the packaged biscuit dough and cut it into quarters. Using three of those quarters, cut the dough into fifteen 1-inch triangles, keeping the last quarter of the dough whole.

3. Cut three of the hot dogs into five pieces each, leaving one whole. Trust me here.

4. Cut three of the pieces of cheese into five strips each, ending up with fifteen strips and a whole slice of cheese.

5. Begin wrapping each piece of hot dog with a strip of cheese, then a piece of the biscuit dough, pulling one of the corners all the way around the hot dog until it touches the dough again so you can seal it on itself.

6. Place with the seam side down onto a baking sheet that has been lightly oiled, or use a nonstick spray. Continue this process until all the hot dogs are wrapped, and use the last large piece of cheese and dough for the whole hot dog.

7. Using the whole hot dog as the body, arrange the smaller pieces around it to build your hot dog monster. As long as the dough is touching another piece of dough, the hot dogs should bake together.

8. Place in the oven for 15 minutes or until golden brown. Allow a few minutes to cool before adding your favorite toppings. Gaze upon the monster of your own creation, and then destroy it via eating.

Animal-Shaped Chicken Nuggets

By Ice King

Blank pages in a cookbook! Ha ha ha! Oh, this is exciting. So exciting I laughed out loud and then wrote that laughter right here. Normal people do that, right? I'm normal?

Anyway, I'm glad I have the opportunity to write down my favorite meal. First step is to buy the Frozen Zoo Fun Chicken Chompers! Then take it out of the box (optional) and put it in the microwave for a while (optional)! Then eat it (mandatory)!

If you cannot find Frozen Zoo Fun Chicken Chompers, you can try to make them on your own. This recipe might work. Good luck.

4 ounces white bread, no crust

1 cup cream

1 ½ pounds chicken breast

¼ cup ice

1 teaspoon salt

1 ½ cups flour

4 eggs

1 tablespoon water

2 cups panko breadcrumbs

2 quarts peanut oil

Animal-shaped cookie cutters

1. Put bread into a bowl. Pour the cream over the bread and allow it to soak up the cream a bit.

2. Cut the chicken breast into small ½-inch cubes and place in a food processor with the ice. Turn on the food processor, gradually adding the pieces of soaked bread to the mixture.

3. Once the bread has been added, slowly add any remaining cream that hasn't been soaked up by the bread. Then add the salt and allow the mixture to completely emulsify and become very smooth. You may need to scrape down the sides of the food processor as you go to ensure the meat is being mixed correctly.

4. Preheat oven to 325°F. Place the meat mixture (called a *farce*) in a greased or nonstick spray-lined bread pan. Tap the whole pan on the counter to help get out any air and spread the mixture as evenly as possible.

5. Cover the bread pan in aluminum foil and place in a casserole dish or pan large enough to hold the bread pan and place in the oven. Before closing the oven, pour enough hot water into the bottom dish to cover half the height of the bread pan. It is important to use hot water; it helps keep the temperatures in the oven up. Cook for 50 to 60 minutes or until the chicken has set in the middle.

6. Set out on counter to cool before transferring to refrigerator for at least 12 hours. Maybe read a long book or look outside at the slow changing of the seasons! Something that lasts 12 hours.

7. Uncover the bread pan and carefully use a knife around the edges to help release the chicken loaf from the pan. Gently turn upside down onto a cutting board and tap on the bottom of the pan, if necessary, to release the chicken from the bottom.

8. Proceed to cut the loaf into ¼-inch thick slices. Once you have sliced the loaf, you can use any animal-shaped cookie cutter to punch out the chicken nuggets.

9. You will need three different bowls to bread the animal shapes. Clean ones! I always forget that. One will be for the flour and another for the eggs and the tablespoon of water, which need to be whisked together. The last bowl is for the breadcrumbs. The chicken shapes need to be covered in the flour and then rolled into the egg wash and dipped straight into the breadcrumbs. The flour sticks to the chicken, and the eggs stick to the flour, and the breadcrumbs stick to the eggs. Once you have covered the chicken in breadcrumbs, place on a plate or baking tray in a single layer. Do not stack.

10. Heat 2 quarts of oil in a 4- to 5-quart pot to 350°F, using a candy thermometer to measure the temperature. When the oil is up to temperature, place the chicken nuggets in the hot oil until golden brown, for 3 to 5 minutes. Only fry a few at time to avoid overcrowding the pot, which can quickly lower the temperature of the oil. When the chicken nuggets are removed from the oil, allow them to drain onto a paper towel and lightly salt them.

OH, MY GLOB. AN UNTAINTED RECIPE FROM OLDEN TIMES FOR LASAGNA! I LOVE PASTA SO MUCH I'M GOING TO JUST KEEP STACKING EVERYTHING UNTIL IT FALLS OVER. —FINN

EIGHT-LAYER LASAGNA

While you may look upon other wives and mothers with envy in front of a mirror, you can now look at them with pity in front of a plate of heavenly lasagna. While they pick at limp salads and watery soups, you will relish a dish of pasta. Winner!

MAKES: 8 servings

IT'S . . . IT'S PERFECT. EVERY LAYER TOGETHER IN HARMONY. AND I CAN FREEZE SQUARES FOR LATER! LIKE A TOMATO-CHEESE ICE CREAM SANDWICH! (OR FOR REHEATING.)

1 pound lean ground beef (93 percent lean)

½ cup small-diced onion

1 quart crushed San Marzano tomatoes

1 teaspoon dried Italian seasoning

1 teaspoon granulated sugar

1 teaspoon chopped garlic

2 cups ricotta cheese

2 cups shredded mozzarella cheese

1 package no-bake lasagna noodles

1. Preheat oven to 375°F. Sauté beef and onion in large skillet until the beef is crumbled and no longer pink. Stir occasionally, allowing the meat to brown.

2. Stir in crushed tomatoes, Italian seasoning, sugar, and garlic. Simmer for 15 to 20 minutes until tomatoes start to break down.

3. Place about a third of the meat sauce over the bottom of a bread loaf pan. Place noodles over meat sauce, top with half of the ricotta cheese and mozzarella cheese, then repeat until 8 layers deep or until you reach the top of the pan.

4. Spray underside of aluminum foil with some cooking spray or grease with a little oil. Cover dish tightly with foil. Bake 30 minutes.

5. Remove foil; bake 15 minutes more or until cheese melts and sauce is bubbly. Let stand 10 minutes before serving.

Oh, wow, chicken, man. I love to catch a tasty chicken. That is a major perk of fox life. Put it in a pie? That is just . . . so wild. I will have to try this soon. I haven't caught a chicken in about two years, though, so maybe I'll just put something else in there instead. Maybe a rusty can.
—Mr. Fox

CHICKEN POT PIE

A fine chicken pot pie is the perfect dish for the single lifestyle. Repeat this recipe four times and eat all the pies at once to celebrate not having to share them with your family members.

MAKES: 1 large pie

1 tablespoon butter	¼ cup flour
1 ½ cups small-diced onion	2 cups chicken stock
1 cup small-diced carrot	½ cup cream
1 cup small-diced celery	½ teaspoon black pepper
1 teaspoon chopped garlic	¼ teaspoon salt
¾ cup green peas	3 cups pulled or diced cooked chicken meat
1 teaspoon chopped fresh thyme	1 can flaky biscuit dough

Okay, I tried it with a rusty can. Not great. Stick with the chicken if you can.

1. Preheat oven to 350°F.

2. In a large-sized pot, melt butter in a skillet over medium-low heat and cook the onion, carrots, celery, and garlic until the celery and carrots are tender (about 15 minutes), stirring occasionally.

3. Stir in peas, thyme, and flour and cook, stirring constantly, until the flour coats the vegetables and begins to fry, about 5 minutes.

4. Whisk in chicken stock and cream and cook until the sauce is thick and bubbling.

5. Season to taste with salt and black pepper and mix in the chicken meat.

6. Transfer the chicken, vegetables, and sauce mixture into a 2-quart baking dish.

7. Arrange biscuits on top of the filling and place in oven for 20 to 25 minutes until top is golden brown.

I found this book under a destroyed tower! I think tricolored tortellini sounds pretty great! Even if combining them causes a massive tower-destroying explosion. It's weird we all just decide to write in a book if we find it! Just some opinions from A-B-D! BYE.
—Abracadaniel

Wizard Battle Tortellini

Makes: 2 servings

By Grand Master Wizard

Aha! Delicious tor-ta-lee-neeee! A fine recipe for a grand archmage to record his most powerful and beloved runes! Readers of the future! Know that *green* tortellini is crucial for this spell! But what will happen if I add beige and red noodles as well?

One 8-ounce bag of cheese tricolor tortellini

½ teaspoon olive oil

1 tablespoon butter

½ cup diced ham

1 tablespoon minced shallot

½ teaspoon minced garlic

Pinch of chili flakes

1 tablespoon white wine

¼ cup green peas

⅓ cup cream

1 tablespoon chopped parsley

1 teaspoon chopped chives

¼ cup shredded Parmesan

1. Bring a large pot of water to a boil and cook the tortellini.

2. Strain the cooked pasta and rinse lightly with cold water. Toss gently with olive oil in a bowl and set aside.

2. In a 10- to 12-inch sauté pan, melt butter on medium-high heat. Add ham, shallot, garlic, and chili flakes, and cook for 4 to 5 minutes, lightly browning the butter.

3. Add wine and cook until it is almost completely evaporated. It will reduce quickly, so add peas and cream quickly.

4. Turn up to high heat and stir well to incorporate all the flavors, allowing sauce to thicken, for 2 to 3 minutes.

5. Add cooked pasta, herbs, and cheese, and cook until they are hot. Be careful not to break the tortellini. Serve immediately.

GRILLED CHEESE AND TOMATO SOUP

Dearest Dad out sick? Mother just home from the hospital where she was under constant surveillance? Serve them this hearty meal for instant benefits!

MAKES: 1 serving

GRILLED CHEESE

2 slices sourdough bread

2 slices sharp cheddar cheese

1 slice Gruyère cheese

1 tablespoon grated Parmesan

1 teaspoon butter

OPTIONAL ADDITIONS:
WHY NOT A HANDFUL OF POTATO CHIPS? —FIONNA

Ooh! Bacon!
Choose bacon! —Cake

APPLES AND BRIE WOULD BE NICE TOO.
—FIONNA

TOMATO SOUP

4 tablespoons unsalted butter

1 tablespoon minced bacon

1 cup small-diced onion

½ cup small-diced carrot

½ cup small-diced celery

4 cloves garlic, minced

5 tablespoons flour

5 cups chicken broth

One 28-ounce can whole, peeled tomatoes

¼ teaspoon dried thyme

1 cup heavy cream

FOR THE GRILLED CHEESE

1. Place the cheese slices in between the sourdough bread, sprinkling some of the Parmesan in between all the layers of cheese.

2. In a medium skillet, melt the butter over medium-high heat and place sandwich in the pan. Sear it on one side for 2 to 3 minutes until bread is golden brown. Flip and repeat until cheese is completely melted and both sides of sandwich are toasted.

FOR THE TOMATO SOUP

1. In a large pot, melt the butter over medium-high heat and add the bacon, cooking it until it is soft and fat is rendered, for 3 to 4 minutes.

2. Add onion, carrot, celery, and garlic and cook on medium heat. When the carrots are just getting soft, add flour, stirring and cooking for about 5 minutes, being careful not to burn it.

3. Pour in the chicken broth, tomatoes, and thyme. Simmer for about 90 minutes, stirring intermittently.

4. Working in batches, begin to transfer the soup to a blender, adding the cream as well and pureeing on high for about 30 seconds to ensure a smooth soup.

5. Bring to a boil again before serving.

I love to illustrate my recipes when I'm not busy stomping out dissent throughout my kingdom. —Ice King

WAIT, YOU'RE ALLOWED TO JUST PUT *CHEESE* IN A SANDWICH AND THEN CALL IT A SANDWICH? NOTHING ELSE? THAT'S ALL I'VE EVER WANTED IN A SANDWICH! JUST MELTED CHEESE! —FIONNA

Girl, you've never heard of grilled cheese? —Cake

IT HAS A NAME? IT EXISTS, AND YOU DIDN'T TELL ME?! —FIONNA

You can . . . dunk it in tomato soup too. —Cake

SILENTLY SCREAMS IN DELIGHT —FIONNA

SIDE DISHES

A COMPLETE MEAL that is both nutritionally diverse and pleasing to
a quickly bored tongue should not merely consist of a simple cut of meat
or hearty bean lopped onto the center of a plate and left in solitude.

Hey, person looking at this book. So, Finn gave me a real sad eye to get me to head up the side dishes section. I think he's trying to get me to confront my French fry issues, which, you know . . . *Fine*. The truth is, I've mostly been enjoying my meals as a big hunk of red with a side of red, washed down with some cool red, and you get the picture. I drink red.

But, like, I remember what it was like to have a nice dinner with a salad or some bright pickles to even out the richness of a heavy meal. In fact, I've heard the boys talk a lot about Prismo's pickles. Maybe we can get those in here. And yes, *I'll do the fries.* (I just yelled this out loud as I wrote it, and Finn clapped and jumped up and down.) –Marceline

Grass Ogre Salad

By Donny

Hey, you! Yeah, you're readin' a book, so that means you're a nerd. What's this?! A buncha recipes! Dummmmb. What's this? Fry a thing? What's that?! Bake a thing?! I don't have time to apply heat to foods! If you try it, you're weird. I bet you tried it a bunch.

Aw, don't get mad! I'm just kidding! You can't take a joke! Geez, you need to stick with me and get a sense of humor. Also, forget that cooking stuff. I mean it. Here's what you do. You take a bunch of stuff out of the ground, and you throw it all in a bowl, and then you put some wet flavored stuff on it so it doesn't dry out your mouth and taste bad.

Dressing

2 teaspoons Dijon mustard

⅓ cup lemon juice

1 tablespoon parsley

1 tablespoon tarragon

1 tablespoon dill

1 tablespoon minced shallot

1 teaspoon honey

1 cup olive oil

Salad

1 cup baby arugula

½ cup baby spinach

1 cup little gem lettuce

1 tablespoon tarragon leaves

1 tablespoon pickled dill

1 tablespoon parsley

2 tablespoons chopped green onion

¼ cup sunflower sprouts

¼ cup thinly sliced cucumber

4 shaved asparagus

¼ cup English peas

FOR THE DRESSING

1. Combine mustard, lemon juice, parsley, tarragon, dill, shallot, and honey in a blender and blend on high speed.
2. Slowly add the olive oil to the blender and then season with salt and pepper.
3. Set the dressing aside and keep refrigerated until use.

FOR ASSEMBLY

1. In a large bowl, combine all of the lettuces, vegetables, herbs, and sprouts. Yeah! All of them! What else did you think you were going to do with all of them, dummy?
2. Add the dressing to the salad mix until coated well and season with salt and pepper.
3. Serve in a large serving bowl or separate into smaller servings on small salad plates. This salad would be great topped with your favorite cheese. It's probably a dumb cheese, though, isn't it? Whatever. Eat what you want, you baby.

Multiverse Pickles By Prisma

Oh! You've made it to my pickle page. Well done. Sorry about Donny back there. I've looked across thousands of realities, and I'm sorry to say there's always going to be a Donny. He might be called "Greg" or "Jenny" or "Your Boss" . . . but he exists across all space and time. So ignore him! Have a pickle. It's sour, and it's crunchy, and it preserves cucumbers, which is a nice thing to do to a cucumber. Also, this recipe contains a secret ritual to bring me back from the dead. Maybe it'll work for you, too? If not, it's still a yummy pickle.

6 pickling cucumbers (preferably Kirby cucumbers)

½ teaspoon coriander seed

¼ teaspoon chili flakes

½ teaspoon yellow mustard seed

½ teaspoon black peppercorns

2 bay leaves

¼ cup salt

6 garlic cloves, halved

6 cups water

2 to 3 whole dill sprigs

1. Place the cleaned and rinsed whole cucumbers in a jar or container that fits them best, with some room to spare for the pickling liquid.

2. Bring the coriander, chili flakes, mustard seed, black peppercorns, bay leaves, salt, garlic, and water to a boil.

3. Cool over an ice bath or refrigerate until completely cold and chilled.

4. Once chilled, pour all those ingredients into the container with the cucumbers, and add the dill. Make sure cucumbers are completely submerged. You know what they say: An unsubmerged cucumber never a pickle shall be.

5. Place in refrigerator for a minimum of 4 to 5 days before tasting. They may take up to 2 to 3 weeks, depending upon the thickness of the cucumbers.

Twisted Macaroni Salad

By Peppermint Butler

I have engaged in unthinkable sorcery with dark beings, it is true. But it is all in service to the Candy Kingdom and Princess Bubblegum. I attend to twisted magic so that she doesn't have to. My methods have a cost, but the results are the harmonious kingdom she deserves. I am her loyal servant. And I have done awful things to acquire this perfect macaroni salad for her. Enjoy.

One 1-pound package
  cavatappi pasta, cooked and chilled

½ cup finely chopped red onion

1 cup sweet relish

¼ cup yellow mustard

¾ teaspoon salt

¼ teaspoon black pepper

4 cups mayonnaise

3 chopped hard-boiled eggs

1. Combine pasta, red onion, sweet relish, mustard, salt, and pepper in a bowl and mix well. Allow to sit refrigerated and covered overnight.

2. Assuming you want to serve the dish in the afternoon or evening, mix 3 cups of mayonnaise into the pasta salad, along with the chopped egg, first thing in the morning.

3. Place back in refrigerator for at least 2 to 3 hours or until serving.

4. Just before serving, add the last cup of mayonnaise and season again with salt and black pepper, if necessary.

Softy Cheese Hot Dogs*

By Jake

Nothing pairs with everything like softy cheese! It's good, like cheese, and it's soft, like most comforting things! I have yet to discover a food I don't like with softy cheese. For you amateurs, though, maybe start out with salty or savory stuff like these hot dogs. Call me when you're ready to go wild with some softy cheese sushi burgers. Heh heh heh.

Oh, and remember Clarence? The guy who ate too much of this stuff, exploded, and became a ghost? Yeah, don't do what he did and explode.

Softy Cheese

¼ cup butter

½ cup small-diced onion

½ cup small-diced carrot

¼ cup small-diced celery

1 teaspoon finely chopped garlic

¼ cup all-purpose flour

½ cup whole milk

1 cup chicken stock

⅓ pound of extra sharp cheddar, shredded

Onion Crunch

1 pint canola oil

1 cup thinly sliced shallots

½ cup all-purpose flour

Pinch of salt

Hot Dogs

10 hot dogs

10 hot dog buns

Pickled jalapeños to taste

*Warning: May cause consumer to **explode!**

FOR THE SOFTY CHEESE

1. In a large saucepan, melt butter on medium-high heat. Add onions, carrots, celery, and garlic, and turn heat down slightly. Cook for 5 to 8 minutes until soft and onions are translucent. Add flour, stirring constantly, evenly coating the vegetables and the pan. Allow to cook for another 4 to 5 minutes, stirring constantly.

2. Add milk and stock, and turn the heat up to high. Bring the mixture to a boil while continuing to stir with a whisk to make sure the flour and liquid are thoroughly combined. As soon as it comes to a boil, turn back to medium heat, stirring and making sure nothing is sticking to the bottom of the pot.

3. Once the sauce starts to thicken, slowly add the cheese until it is all melted into the space. Once the cheese is melted, you can transfer to a blender to puree the sauce thoroughly on high until very smooth. Set aside or refrigerate for later use.

FOR THE ONION CRUNCH

1. In a medium saucepan, heat the oil to 300°F. In a mixing bowl, toss the shallots and flour together. Coat the shallots thoroughly in the flour, breaking the shallot layers apart as you incorporate the flour in order to fully coat the shallots.

2. Use a strainer to sift the excess flour on the shallots and, in about two or three batches, carefully place the shallots into the hot oil. The shallots are done when they are golden brown and crispy. (Generally, when you don't see any more bubbles around the shallots, they're good to go.)

3. Shallots should be pulled from oil with a slotted spoon and laid on paper towels to strain excess oil. Lightly salt so the seasoning sticks to them before they cool down.

FOR THE HOT DOGS

1. Heat oven to 300°F. Cook hot dogs on medium heat, about half covered with water, in a large saucepan, covered, for 10 minutes.

2. When the hot dogs are about halfway cooked, throw the buns on a baking sheet in the oven. That way, the buns and dogs will be ready at the same time.

3. For assembly: Grab a bun and a hot dog. Add as much softy cheese and jalapeños to your dog as you please, and finish it off with some onion crunch for the best hot dog ever.

Grass Sword Spicy Green Beans

Makes: 4 servings

By Jake

Okay, so, uh, we got a green bean recipe here. Now, I like green beans, but I understand they usually take a little bit of salesmanship. So, here's what you do. You take your cooked green beans, and you make 'em into little swords, just like Finn's grass sword! Then you wage great battle upon your hunger! Sword after sword down the gullet, fighting the terrible hunger beast and the beast of poor nutrition! And after that, if it turns out you still don't like green beans—hey, at least you tried.

¼ cup miso paste

1 tablespoon gochujang
   (red chili paste)

2 tablespoons finely chopped
   green onion

1 clove garlic, minced

¼ cup minced onion

2 teaspoons honey

2 teaspoons sesame oil

2 teaspoons toasted sesame seeds

1 teaspoon grated ginger

2 tablespoons vegetable oil

1 pound green beans,
   stemmed and halved

1. In a medium mixing bowl, add the miso paste, gochujang, green onion, garlic, onion, honey, sesame oil, sesame seeds, and ginger. Mix these ingredients until well combined and set aside.

2. In a large frying pan, add the vegetable oil and turn on high heat. Wait until the oil is just lightly smoking, and add the green beans quickly. Be careful not to splash the hot oil.

3. Sauté the green beans, stirring frequently, until the green beans are blistered but not browning or burning. When cooking with such high heat, move the pan slightly off or above the heat to control the temperature as opposed to changing the temperature manually, as this is a quick process and should only take 2 to 3 minutes.

4. Once you have cooked the beans to this point, add the sauce you made.

5. Continue to cook on high heat until beans are coated with sauce and are tender but not soft and mushy. Serve right away while the dish is still very hot.

DON'T FORGET THE SWORD PART! — Jake

Lumpy Smashed Potato Salad

By Lumpy Space Princess

Ugh! Where's the artistry in this book? Where's the glamour? It's all just a bunch of stuff to put in your eating hole. This book needs a recipe to aspire to . . . something beautiful. That's why this next recipe is a way to make an edible sculpture of yours truly.

1 ½ pounds sweet potato (dark skin, white flesh), medium-diced

¼ cup small-diced red bell pepper

¼ cup small-diced celery

¼ cup small-diced red onion

¼ cup small-diced pickled peppadew peppers

½ cup chopped cilantro

½ cup fresh lime juice

¼ cup olive oil

½ teaspoon salt

½ teaspoon black pepper

1. To blanch sweet potatoes, start with cold water and diced sweet potatoes in a large pot; there should be at least enough water to cover double the height of the potatoes or more. Don't let the water come to a complete boil. It should be simmering with only a little bit of water surface movement. This process is a more tempered way to make sure the potatoes cook evenly. You're welcome! Hint: Sometimes a heavy boiling pot can result in a potato perfectly cooked on the inside and soft on the outside. Now you know!

2. Once the sweet potatoes are tender and have cooled completely, toss the other ingredients together with the sweet potatoes.

3. Fold gently until thoroughly combined. Season to taste.

Wait, where are the beans?! They're like a staple or something. I'm gonna need a few more pages, Finn.

—Lumpy Space Princess

Lumpy Baked Beans

By Lumpy Space Princess

Oh my glob, you're already done with that last one?! Fine, since you're, like, some wannabe cooking person, here's how to make my beans. You can show your loser parents that you are doing awesome on your own.

1 pound dried navy beans, rinsed

¼ pound bacon, small-diced

1 cup small-diced onion

½ cup dark brown sugar

¼ cup molasses

⅓ cup apple cider vinegar

1 tablespoon mustard powder

¼ teaspoon black pepper

5 cups water

½ teaspoon salt

1. In a 6-quart slow cooker, add beans, bacon, onion, brown sugar, molasses, vinegar, mustard powder, black pepper, and water.

2. Cover and set on low to cook for 12 hours until the liquid is nice and thick. If it seems too thin, uncover after 12 hours and let simmer with the lid off for about another hour. If you're doing this in the woods, keep an eye on it. Animals love to steal my beans!

3. Once the beans have reached a desired consistency, add the salt to finish seasoning, and they're ready to go.

Lumpy White Beans

By Lumpy Space Princess

Makes: 10 servings

Ah! Just like home. Lumpy, lumpy kind of bean-smelling home. Rub these beans on your face to make your skin look good like mine.

1 pound Great Northern white beans

¼ cup olive oil

1 cup small-diced onions

½ cup small-diced celery

1 tablespoon chopped garlic

1 tablespoon chopped thyme

2 teaspoons chopped oregano

¼ teaspoon black pepper

¼ teaspoon ground cumin

Pinch of cayenne

6 cups water

½ teaspoon salt

1. In a 6-quart slow cooker, add beans, olive oil, onion, celery, garlic, thyme, oregano, black pepper, cumin, cayenne, and water.

2. Cover and set on low to cook for 12 hours until the liquid is nice and thick. If it seems too thin, uncover after 12 hours and let simmer with the lid off for about an hour. Again, don't let animals steal it as you do so.

3. Once the beans have reached a desired consistency, add the salt to finish seasoning, and they're ready to go.

73

Lich King Poppers

By Lich King

Reader. Do not turn the page. Do not look away. You have found a remnant of the never-dying, never-living Lich . . . Even in this grimoire of old, dedicated to providing nutrients to the living in fun, delicious forms, I am here, ever present. I will return in more substantial form, but, until then, consume these crispy, cheesy jalapeño poppers and think of me.

Let the spice that hurts your tongue remind you that I will burn all I see, and I will see all.

12 jalapeños

1 tablespoon vegetable oil

8 ounces cream cheese

¼ cup chopped green onion

¼ cup corn

1 lime, juiced and zested

1 ½ cups flour

3 eggs, beaten with 1 tablespoon water

2 cups panko breadcrumbs

4 cups peanut oil

Use green jalapeños so it looks kind of like me. See you soon . . .

1. Preheat oven to 350°F.

2. Toss the jalapeños in the vegetable oil and roast in oven on a baking sheet for 10 minutes.

3. Once they're out of the oven, place in a bowl and cover tightly with plastic wrap or a sealed lid. Allow to cool, covered, for about 20 minutes. This allows the peppers to continue to cook so that the flesh will soften and be easier to work with. In the meantime, prepare the filling and breading ingredients.

4. In a small bowl, combine the cream cheese, green onion, corn, and lime juice and zest and mix until thoroughly combined.

5. Place cheese mixture in a piping/pastry bag or a ziplock bag you can cut a corner from to use like a pastry bag.

6. Breading the peppers will require four bowls or containers: one for the flour, one for the beaten eggs, one for the breadcrumbs, and the last for the peppers once they are nice and coated with breading.

7. Once cool to the touch, the peppers' skins should peel right off.

8. After the skin is peeled, carefully cut a slit on one side from the stem to the tip of the pepper. Then gently take the seeds out.

9. Carefully fill the peppers with the cheese mixture, making sure they stay close to their original shape.

10. Carefully coat each pepper in the flour; then coat completely in the egg mixture and then in the breadcrumbs. It is important to take the time to coat the peppers thoroughly during each step to ensure proper cooking results. The coating will seal the peppers to keep the cheese from coming out.

11. After the peppers have been breaded, place in refrigerator for an hour if you are cooking them immediately. Otherwise, they will hold best in the freezer until you are ready to fry them.

12. In a 3-quart saucepan, heat the peanut oil to 350°F, using a candy thermometer to check temperature.

13. Gently drop the poppers into the oil one at a time and fry for 2 to 3 minutes, until golden brown. If frozen, they may take 4 to 5 minutes.

Marceline's Fries

By Marceline

When I was a kid, I lived with my dad for awhile. And one night I bought these French fries! I ate one, and it was amazing. I had to go outside for a sec. I don't remember why, but when I got back, I found that my totally evil dad had eaten the rest.

Ever since then I've been chasing a fry recipe that could re-create the flavor of that fry . . . and have yet to find it. I've come to recognize that what might make something taste perfect is the context of the moment.

So, make these fries. Eat one. Savor it. Love it. You'll find that it will remain in your memory as the greatest fry you've ever eaten.

2 pounds russet potatoes

3 quarts peanut oil for frying

One 12-ounce bottle Tajín

½ cup mayonnaise

½ cup sour cream

½ cup Cotija cheese

2 tablespoons lime juice

¼ teaspoon black pepper

½ teaspoon garlic powder

1 teaspoon Dijon mustard

1. Cut potatoes lengthwise into slices ¼-inch-thick, and then cut each slice lengthwise into slices ¼-inch-thick again, keeping the pieces as long as possible.

2. Soak all of the cut potatoes in cold water for 2 to 3 hours.

3. Rinse the potatoes out in a colander and allow to thoroughly drain of excess water.

4. Use a 6-quart (or larger) heavy-bottomed saucepan to heat the frying oil. Make sure the oil only fills the bottom half of the pan so you don't fry your fingers instead of the potatoes.

5. Heat the oil to 300°F, using a candy thermometer to measure temperature. The French fries will be cooked in two steps for very crispy results.

6. Cook the fries in batches for 3 to 4 minutes at a time, allowing each batch to drain onto paper towels.

7. Once you have partially cooked the fries and allowed them to drain, cool them in the fridge for at least 30 minutes.

8. Once you're ready to eat, cook the fries a second time, this time in oil at 375°F. As long as you don't overcrowd the pot, you will end up with super crispy fries.

9. As soon as the fries are ready, toss them in a bowl with Tajín to taste.

10. Combine mayonnaise, sour cream, Cotija cheese, lime juice, black pepper, garlic powder, and mustard in a bowl and mix ingredients thoroughly. Use as a dip for the fries.

Beverages

DON'T TELL THE MAYOR, but the editors of this publication believe that old-fashioned water simply doesn't always do the trick when it comes to hydration! Of course you must get your eight glasses per day, but why not slip in some flavor now and then? (If you don't tell the mayor.)

GREETINGS! I, THE EARL OF LEMONGRAB, have been given the duty of introducing the beveraaaaageesss!! Did they believe I would provide the secret to LEMONADE? Bah! It is but sugar, lemon, and water! Don't write it down! It's too easy! TOOOOO EAAAAAASY!

Hm. There are other drinks. A grape drink. A chocolate drink. A honey drink. A bug drink. They are all . . . ACCEPTAAAAAAABLLLEEE!

Now I will hand the book to Marceline, who will teach you how to make Super Porp. —Earl of Lemongrab

Super Porp
81

Fruity Punch From That One Dream You Had
82

Bug Milk
83

Hot Cocoa
85

Honey Energy Drink
87

Super Porp

By Marceline

Makes: 16 servings

Man, Super Porp was around forever. But they don't really make it anymore. Something must have happened at the factory. Anyway, I did some messing around, and this should replicate its hyperaddictive flavor.

1 gallon tea, brewed hot

1 cup sugar

½ cup store-bought kombucha

1 kombucha starter SCOBY

1 quart Concord grape juice

1. Add the sugar to the tea while the tea is hot. That way, it dissolves before it cools.

2. Pour the tea solution and store-bought kombucha into a very clean 1-gallon glass jar.

3. With very clean hands, place the SCOBY in the jar. It should float, but don't worry if it sinks at first.

4. Cover the jar with a cloth or a coffee filter and secure it with rubber bands around the top of the jar. Super Porp needs to breathe.

5. Allow to sit in a warm spot in the kitchen for 6 to 9 days. You have made kombucha, but in order for it to carbonate and turn into Super Porp kombucha soda, you will need to do a second fermentation step.

6. Pour the grape juice into a separate, very clean 1-gallon glass jar. Fill the rest of the jar with the kombucha base, leaving about an inch of space at the top of the jar.

7. Cover the jar tightly with its lid and allow to sit at room temperature for 5 days. Serve chilled or over ice.

8. You can start another batch using the same SCOBY and replacing the store-bought kombucha in the recipe with the leftover kombucha you now have.

Hey, remember the super Porp jingle?

Super Porp, it hits the spot.
It messes up your train of thought.
If you're thirsty and out of shape,
Get down on that fizzy grape.

Super Porp.

—Marceline

Fruity Punch From That One Dream You Had

By Cosmic Owl

I've looked inside a lot of people's dreams (it's kind of my thing), and I see a lot of other punch ingredients pop up in dreams about parties! Weird, I know, but in case you forget, here's what your subconscious probably wants in your punch: carrot discs, endless lemons, surprisingly sweet tears, leftover previous punch, and even a blend of club soda and seltzer.

3 cups water

1 quart strawberries, cleaned and stemmed

3 cups sugar

One 48-ounce can pineapple juice

Two 6-ounce cans orange juice concentrate, thawed

Two 6-ounce cans lemonade concentrate, thawed

1 quart lemon-lime soda

1. In a large pot, add the water, strawberries, and sugar and bring to a boil, stirring to make sure sugar doesn't stick to bottom of pot.

2. Immediately turn off and transfer to a blender a little bit at a time, making sure not to fill the blender up more than halfway. Puree until smooth.

3. Strain through a fine mesh strainer and allow to cool completely.

4. In a large punch bowl or bucket, add the rest of the ingredients and the strawberry mixture and mix until combined. Serve chilled over ice. Drink right before bedtime if you want a weird dream about it.

Bug Milk

by Hunson Abadeer

Heeeey, so here's how to make bug milk. It's a little recipe I'd like to keep around because it's a crucial ingredient for freeing me from the Nightosphere. Yeah, just draw a happy face on any surface, say some simple incantations, pour this around, and you'll be doing your pal Hunson a big favor.

Don't tell anyone I snuck this into the book.

½ cup raw peanuts

½ cup toasted peanuts

⅓ cup cocoa powder

1 tablespoon agave

Pinch of salt

4 cups water

1. First, make a classic nut milk, which can be made with any nut (almond, pistachio, walnut, hazelnut, etc.). This recipe uses ½ cup of toasted peanuts for flavor, but generally nut milks are only made with raw nuts. Soak the raw peanuts and toasted peanuts in enough water to cover by a couple of inches. Allow to soak, covered, overnight for a minimum of 12 hours.

2. Discard the water in which the nuts are soaking.

3. Place nuts in a blender along with the cocoa powder, agave, and salt.

4. Bring 4 cups of water to just under a boil, around 180°F, and pour into the blender as well.

5. Start blender on low, gradually increasing speed until blender is on high. Blend for 2 to 3 minutes.

6. Pour through a fine sieve, pressing on the pulp to push all liquid through the sieve. Discard any of the leftover pulp.

7. Store in an airtight container in the refrigerator. Serve Bug Milk nice and cold . . . or draw a smiley face and pour this drink on the ground.

No actual bugs. Pretty good trick, huh? HA HA HA! —Hunson Abadeer

HOT COCOA

Snowmen. Sledding. Seasonal depression. All important and often unavoidable elements of the winter months. But no snowy day would be complete without a rich cup of hot chocolate. Pour this essential chocolatey confection into your favorite mug and settle in for a long, dark winter.

MAKES: 1 serving

2 tablespoons cocoa powder

1 ½ tablespoons sugar

Pinch of salt

10 fluid ounces milk

¼ teaspoon vanilla extract

2 tablespoons marshmallow fluff

1. In a 12-ounce coffee mug or glass, mix the cocoa, sugar, and salt.

2. In a small saucepan, heat milk and vanilla on medium-high heat until you see bubbles forming around the edges of the pot.

3. Pour half the milk mixture into the glass and stir thoroughly to dissolve the dry ingredients.

4. Once dissolved, pour in the last half of the milk and stir until combined.

5. Top your hot cocoa off with a heaping scoop of marshmallow fluff.

You did it! Drink it! Yay! —BMO

Honey Energy Drink

By Party Pat

Makes: 4 servings

Listen, we know the Chief parties pretty crazy. Like that party in the stomach of a giant monster. That is how crazy my party game is. But it takes more than an eye sticker and a karaoke machine to party with the Chief. You need to drink the honey drink to party all the time.

3 cups coconut water

1 cup water

1 tablespoon cider vinegar

3 tablespoons honey

1 cup strawberries, stemmed

½ teaspoon fresh grated ginger

Juice of 1 lemon

¼ teaspoon salt

1. Place all the ingredients into a blender. Turn the blender on low and slowly increase the speed to highest setting. Allow to run for 30 seconds on high and then turn off.

2. Either strain through a fine sieve to get rid of some of the pulp or leave it as is. This drink is best served nice and cold.

DESSERTS

AND WHAT IS A MEAL WITHOUT a sweet reminder of life's pleasures at the end? From decadent to creamy, here are desserts for you to sample.

This is my JAM! Sweet stuff, what up!

Cakes! Ice cream! Chips! ICE CREAM AGAIN! This is my lifeblood, guys. Some of these are fun little treats for yourself, for yourself-times. Others are nice for a crowd! Have a little party with Finn Cakes! Freak out the squares by sticking potato chips in ice cream! And, of COURSE, we have gotten kindly Tree Trunks to provide her famous apple pie. Enjoy! THIS IS THE BEST PART OF THE BOOK. Also, it looks like this book has been passed around for a LONG time since Finn last saw it. I'll hand it off to him so he can add some Finn Cakes and check in. —Princess Bubblegum

OH MY GLOB, THEY LOOK JUST LIKE ME! —FINN

Finn Cakes
BY FINN

Oh man! This book is coming together nicely! I feel good about it. It feels like a nice community tribute to my mom now.

But onto the cakes. These cakes are very special to me. They have my face, and they taste real nice. I feel a connection with them, you know? Anyway, if you want to eat my tiny soft head in a totally noncreepy way, this is the way to do it! I do it all the time!

Sometimes these don't come out looking exactly like me, which is okay! I pretend they are terrible clones who need to be . . . dealt with.

Cupcakes

1 ½ cups all-purpose flour

1 cup sugar

1 teaspoon baking soda

1 teaspoon salt

½ cup cocoa powder

1 cup water

1 whole egg

½ cup vegetable oil

1 teaspoon vinegar

40 small marshmallows (reserve for decoration)

Buttercream Frosting

½ cup butter, softened

4 ½ cups powdered sugar

1 ½ teaspoons vanilla extract

¼ cup whole milk

2 teaspoons cocoa powder (for decorating a handsome boy's fondant face)

Fondant

½ cup light corn syrup

½ cup shortening

¼ teaspoon salt

½ teaspoon clear vanilla extract

1 pound powdered sugar

Red food coloring

FOR THE CUPCAKES

1. Preheat oven to 350°F.
2. Combine dry ingredients (flour, sugar, baking soda, salt, cocoa powder) in a large bowl and gently mix to combine. In a separate bowl, whisk together wet ingredients (water, egg, oil, vinegar).
3. Add wet ingredients to the dry ones while slowly whisking until the batter becomes smooth and lump-free. Scrape the batter out into a measuring cup or pitcher—something pourable to fill the cupcake liners with ease.
4. Spray cupcake pans with a coating of nonstick spray. Insert a liner into each mold, and spray them as well.
5. Fill the cupcake molds with batter up to about ¼-inch from the top of the liners. Tap and rattle the trays to get out any air bubbles stuck in the batter.
6. Bake for 15 to 18 minutes. Test by inserting a wooden skewer or toothpick into the center of the cake. If it comes out clean, the cake is done baking.
7. Allow cupcakes to cool for about 15 minutes in cupcake pans. When cool enough to take out, place cakes on a rack or counter for 2 hours to finish cooling completely before decorating.

FOR THE BUTTERCREAM FROSTING

1. In a mixing bowl large enough to hold all the ingredients, place softened butter, powdered sugar, vanilla extract, and milk.
2. Whip the ingredients with a hand mixer until light and airy. Place frosting in a bowl.
3. Take ¼ cup of frosting and place in a separate, small mixing bowl. Add the cocoa powder to frosting and whisk gently until smooth. Place the chocolate frosting into a piping bag for creating my (Finn's) facial features.
4. The rest of the frosting is for the white hat (which will eventually get marshmallow ears) that covers my head, except for my face. Apply a generous ¼-inch coat of frosting in one even, smooth layer using an offset spatula. Hold on to that chocolate frosting for finishing touches. Refrigerate until ready to finish decorating.

FOR THE FONDANT

1. In a large mixing bowl, use a wooden spoon to mix the corn syrup and shortening until combined.

2. Add salt and vanilla to the mixture and mix until completely smooth.

3. Mix in the powdered sugar and knead until very smooth and slightly dry to the touch.

4. Add food coloring in very small increments until you have reached desired color (a light pink hue to give Finn's face some color). If need be, add small amounts of powdered sugar until consistency is good.

5. Using a rolling pin, roll the fondant out to $\frac{1}{16}$-inch thickness. Roll out the fondant in two separate batches to make it easier to work with.

6. Cut out rounds using a ring cutter. Use the edge of the ring cutter to punch the rounds of fondant slightly off center, removing a sliver of the round and leaving you with the offset (oval) shape of my face.

7. Place one fondant face on the bottom third of each cupcake top.

8. Use marshmallows for the ears on my hat.

9. Cut a small hole in the tip of the pastry bag and practice using it a little. Then use the chocolate frosting to make two beady eyes and a mouth on each fondant face.

10. Cupcakes should be stored in a closed or sealed container in the refrigerator if not being served within a few hours. They are best served at room temperature.

LEMON BARS

Don't let the sour fruit of your meager circumstances get you down! When life gives you lemons, you can make lemon bars with this fabulous lemon bar recipe! Of course, life has to also give you flour, sugar, butter, and eggs. And, frankly, that doesn't seem likely.

MAKES: 18 bars

CRUST	FILLING	
2 cups flour	1 ½ cups sugar	Powdered sugar for decorating
½ cup sugar	¼ cup flour	10 lemon drop candies
¼ teaspoon salt	4 large eggs	
1 cup cold butter, small diced	5 lemons, juiced and zested	

FOR THE CRUST

1. Preheat oven to 350°F.

2. Butter a 9- x 13-inch baking dish and place in refrigerator.

3. In a large mixing bowl, place flour, sugar, salt, and butter.

4. Work the mixture with your hands, breaking the butter into the flour and crumbling it through your hands until you have a fine crumble.

5. Pour the crumble into the baking dish and evenly press the dough firmly into the bottom, covering it evenly.

6. Bake for 18 to 20 minutes or until golden brown.

7. Set aside to cool while you prepare the lemon filling. Make sure it is cool, or you will suffer!

FOR THE FILLING

1. Whisk together the sugar and flour, and then add eggs, continuing to whisk until everything is well combined.

2. Add lemon juice and zest and whisk together.

3. Pour filling into the baking dish, covering the crust.

4. Bake for 20 minutes.

5. Refrigerate for 3 hours and then sift powdered sugar over the top. Slice into whatever size bars you like in the pan and carefully slide out with a spatula.

6. Just before serving, place lemon drop candies in a small plastic bag. Smash them into a fine crumble and sprinkle over the lemon bars.

Lady Rainicorn / Lord Monochromicorn Bundt Cake

By Ice King

This cake represents a beautiful romance that can only exist in a land of fantasy. Lady Rainicorn. Lord Monochromicorn. Two perfect opposites flying in an unbroken ring.

Cake

1 pound cold butter

6 cups sugar

6 eggs

4 cups all-purpose flour

1 cup milk

1 teaspoon vanilla extract

¼ cup colored sprinkles

¼ cup flour

¾ cup cocoa powder

Lemon Glaze

2 cups powered sugar

2 tablespoons lemon juice

1 tablespoon lemon zest

FOR THE CAKE

1. Preheat oven to 300°F. Heavily grease a Bundt pan with butter and then coat with flour.

2. In a large bowl, beat butter with an electric or stand mixer on medium speed. Gradually add sugar, mixing until light in color and fluffy.

3. Beat in eggs one at a time. Gradually add flour alternately with the milk, then mix in vanilla extract.

4. Split the batter in half and add the sprinkles to one of the halves and the cocoa powder to the other. Pour the batters into opposite sides of the pan at the same time.

5. Bake for 1 hour and 40 minutes, or until a toothpick inserted in the center comes out clean.

6. Cool in pan for 10 to 15 minutes, then remove and place on a wire rack.

FOR THE LEMON GLAZE

1. Mix all the ingredients together into a smooth paste. If glaze feels too thick, add ½ teaspoon of water at a time until desired consistency is reached.

2. Use this to glaze the Bundt cake.

Hey, what is this? Who's making cakes about my lady and some other horse dude I've never met?! Shut it down! — Jake

Ice King Sundae

By Ice King

Hee hee, oh golly, a treat as cold as the Ice Kingdom itself! Tastes better, though. Do I have to write that? Yes, this ice cream tastes better than going out and eating bits and pieces of frozen landscape. Ice King, this is a memo to yourself.

½ cup whipping cream

1 tablespoon sugar

3 ice cream cones

¼ cup butterscotch sauce

1 pint vanilla (or blueberry) ice cream

¼ cup chocolate fudge sauce

2 tablespoons salted and roasted crushed peanuts

3 maraschino cherries

1. In a medium bowl, whisk together the whipping cream and sugar until it is a thick whipped cream. Set aside in refrigerator until ready to use.

2. Take two ice cream cones and carefully break the top halves off in pieces. Chop up those pieces to about the same size as the peanuts. Mix together and set aside.

3. Cover the bottom of a large cereal bowl with butterscotch sauce.

4. Place four large scoops of ice cream in the bowl next, followed by the chocolate fudge sauce.

5. Place the large cone with the bottom point sticking up in the middle and the two now-shorter cones on either side to look like my crown. Neat, huh?

6. Top with the whipped cream and mixed peanuts with chopped cone crumble. Add the cherries to resemble the gems in my precious, precious crown. Don't go crazy! HA HA HA! Gunter, no! Don't eat it!

Pink and Fluffy Cream Puffs

By Prince Gumball

Friends, it's Prince Gumball again. I'm gonna be real with you. One time I made a batch of these. Then they grew batwings, flew off, and were an impossible nuisance throughout the Candy Kingdom for years. Years of cream filling plopped all over the place, you understand? And then another time I made a batch with the Fluffy People, only for Marshall Lee to suck the color out of them. Enjoy these cream puffs at your peril.

Pastry

½ cup butter, cut into 1-inch cubes

1 teaspoon sugar

½ teaspoon salt

1 cup water

1 cup flour

5 large eggs

Cream

2 cups cream

2 tablespoons sugar

¼ teaspoon vanilla

Red food coloring

FOR THE PASTRY

1. Preheat oven to 375°F.
2. Bring butter, sugar, salt, and water to a boil. As soon as the mixture begins to boil, add flour and stir for 2 minutes on high heat.
3. Transfer to a bowl and let sit for about 1 minute.
4. Add 4 of the eggs, one at a time, whisking to completely incorporate each egg before adding the next.
5. Let sit for 5 minutes to cool slightly. Transfer to a pastry bag with a ½-inch to a ⅝-inch plain round tip.

FOR THE CREAM

1. Whip together cream, sugar, and vanilla with a whisk or stand mixer until it is nice and stiff.
2. Carefully add a small amount of red food coloring to color the whipped cream pink.
3. Transfer to a pastry bag with a plain round tip and keep cold.

FOR ASSEMBLY

1. Prepare a baking sheet lined with parchment paper.
2. Pipe out 2-inch rounds of the pastry about 2 inches apart from each other, and gently smooth the tops of the rounds with a wet finger.
3. Create an egg wash by beating together the last egg with a tablespoon of water until well combined. Brush the tops of each pastry with egg wash.
4. Bake for 30 minutes until golden brown. Allow to cool on a rack.
5. Once the puffs are cool, it is time to fill them with the whipped cream. Gently insert pastry bag tip into the pastry, being careful not to go through the other side. Fill each cream puff slowly, pulling out and filling it up at the same time. Enjoy!

Royal Tart

By Peppermint Butler

In the kingdom of Ooo, only one dessert is amazing enough to kill for: the royal tart. I cannot possibly share the real recipe for the tart only fit for royalty. It is not as if you will ever merit an invitation to the back-rubbing ceremony, even as a tart toter. This version of the royal tart should suffice for your peasant tongue.

1 ½ cups flour

½ teaspoon salt

⅓ cup sugar

⅓ cup cold butter, small diced

2 tablespoons cold shortening

3 tablespoons cold water

8 ounces cream cheese

¼ cup sugar

¼ teaspoon vanilla

Zest of 1 lemon

1 ½ pounds strawberries, halved

¼ cup seedless strawberry jam

1. Preheat oven to 425°F.

2. Using a food processor, combine flour, salt, and sugar by pulsing a few times. Add butter and shortening and pulse another 6 or 7 times until mixture has a crumbly consistency. While running the processor, add water 1 tablespoon at a time until it forms a ball. Add more water slowly as necessary.

3. Cover the dough in plastic wrap and refrigerate for an hour.

4. While the dough is resting, make the filling. In a medium bowl, combine the cream cheese, sugar, vanilla, and lemon zest and whisk until smooth.

5. Once tart dough has rested, use a rolling pin to roll out the dough into a circle about ⅛-inch thick. Lay it over a 9-inch tart pan. Be sure to press the dough into the bottom and sides of the tart pan. Place in freezer for about 15 minutes.

6. Prick the dough several times all over with a fork.

7. Bake for 25 to 30 minutes, or until golden brown. Halfway through, use the back of a spoon to press down the center of the tart, ensuring it doesn't rise too much.

8. Allow dough to cool completely in the tart pan, then spread the filling evenly across the tart.

9. Place strawberries upright around the tart in rings, until it is filled all the way to the center.

10. Heat strawberry jam in a saucepan until it is warm and loose. Brush across the strawberries, glazing the whole tart. Serve immediately. If you're planning on serving it later, then why did you bother with the hot strawberry jam? See, this is why I can't show you the real version.

This recipe probably should go in the Breakfast section, but frankly, Breakfast Princess has enough power already. So I've added jelly beans to create the ultimate dessert jelly. If you don't have the ability to project jelly beans at will (which I understand is typical), perhaps a store can provide the jelly beans? I've never had to try, personally.

—Princess Bubblegum

JELLY BEAN JELLY

Do you find yourself dreading a breakfast of plain, dry toast? Find yourself breaking into hysterical sobs at the thought of filmy butter on a piece of boring wheat bread? Then allow Founders' Island to introduce the wonders of jelly!

MAKES: 24 servings

4 cups white grape juice

3 cups sugar

6 ounces liquid pectin

4 cups jelly beans

1. In a large pot, bring grape juice and sugar to a boil.

2. Stir in pectin. And jelly beans!

3. Continue to boil for 1 minute and then remove from heat and transfer to a jar.

4. Allow to cool to room temperature before refrigerating.

NOTE: White grape juice is very neutral in flavor, so pick your favorite jelly bean flavor to make whichever kind of jelly you want.

Chips & Ice Cream

Transcribed by BMO

Chips! Ice cream. Chips chips chips chips chips chips chips.
Ice cream? Ice cream ice cream. Chips! chips!

1 pint of ice cream

One 14-ounce bag of plain potato chips

3 cups diced strawberries

½ cup sugar

Juice of 1 lemon

1. Place ice cream in medium-size scoops on a cookie sheet or casserole dish. Freeze for at least 2 hours.

ICE CREAM!

2. Crush potato chips to about the size of peas in a bowl and set aside.

CHIPS CHIPS!

3. In a small saucepan on medium heat, mix 2 cups of strawberries and the sugar and lemon juice. Cook until strawberries are completely soft, about 10 minutes.

4. Turn off the heat and immediately add in the rest of the strawberries, stirring to combine.

5. Transfer to another bowl. Put in refrigerator to cool.

6. To serve, roll ice cream, one scoop at a time, in the potato chips until completely coated.

7. Place each scoop in a bowl and surround with strawberry sauce. Consider adding a few fresh strawberries as well!

Ooo-Famous Apple Pie

Makes: 1 pie

BY TREE TRUNKS

Oh, my, yes, of course your older good friend Tree Trunks would be pleased to share her most famous pie recipe. I love to see how much people enjoy it, so to know it will be shared across generations of sweet pie-seekers gives me no end of delight.

I've also got a fun variation, inspired by that time I was a *power-mad goddess of crystal power.*

3 apples, peeled, cored, and
   sliced thin

3 tablespoons sugar

2 tablespoons flour

1 teaspoon vanilla extract

1 teaspoon apple pie spice

Pinch of salt

One 15-ounce package prepared
   raw pie crust

1 tablespoon milk

1 egg, beaten

1. Preheat oven to 375°F. Prepare a lightly greased baking sheet.
2. In a bowl, toss together the apples, sugar, flour, vanilla, pie spice, and salt, coating the apples well in all the other ingredients.
3. Lay out pie dough carefully onto greased baking sheet.
4. Brush a thin layer of milk on the pie dough.
5. Place apples on only half of the dough, also leaving a 1-inch border around the edges.
6. Carefully fold the other half of the dough over the apples and pinch the edges together at the border, sealing the apples in the dough.
7. Cut a few slits on the top of the pie and brush a thin layer of the beaten egg wash over the top.
8. Bake for 45 minutes.
9. Let cool for 10 minutes and serve warm or let sit and serve at room temperature.

Minerva Feast

BY FINN

Wow, only a little bit of blank space left in this book! I really gotta give it up to all my friends and . . . okay, I guess a couple of enemies. I don't know who ghost-wrote them, but there are some Fionna and Cake recipes too! Everybody really came together to help make this book of my mom's really have a life again! I think one last recipe ought to do it.

Ingredients

Choose one recipe from each section.

PREP TIME: ABOUT
A DAY, TO BE SAFE

1. YOU CAN MAKE EVERY RECIPE IN THE BOOK FOR THE ULTIMATE FEAST! OR PICK ONE RECIPE FROM EACH SECTION TO CREATE A MASSIVE FEAST IN YOUR MOM'S HONOR. GET A LITTLE TEARY ON THE MOM THING AND THEN FREAK OUT BECAUSE COOKING ALL THIS FOOD WILL BE SO MUCH WORK!

2. Hey! No freaking out over the promise of the biggest/best meal of all time! Get your friends to help out, dude! Just like with the new additions to this book! Everybody handles a little bit. —Jake

3. HEH, THANKS BUDDY. EVERYONE, MAKE YOUR OWN RECIPE, AND COME TOGETHER FOR A POTLUCK! CONSIDERING THERE ARE SECTIONS THAT COVER EVERYTHING FROM BREAKFAST TO DESSERT, THIS PARTY COULD GO ON FOR A WHILE!

4. SERVE IMMEDIATELY, AT THE VARIOUS TEMPERATURES REQUIRED. FEEL GOOD KNOWING THAT MINERVA AND THE ANCIENT HUMAN DINING SYSTEM LIVE ON IN EACH GOOEY, CRUNCHY, OR OTHERWISE TASTY BITE. YEAH, EVEN IN THE ICE KING'S YEEARGH!

INSIGHT
EDITIONS

PO Box 3088
San Rafael, CA 94912
www.insighteditions.com

Find us on Facebook: www.facebook.com/InsightEditions
Follow us on Twitter: @insighteditions

CARTOON
NETWORK

™ & © Cartoon Network. (s16)

Library of Congress Cataloging-in-Publication Data available.

ISBN: 978-1-60887-643-3

Publisher: Raoul Goff
Acquisitions Manager: Robbie Schmidt
Art Director: Chrissy Kwasnik
Designer: Jon Glick
Executive Editor: Vanessa Lopez
Associate Editor: Katie DeSandro
Production Editorial Manager: Alan Kaplan
Production Editor: Elaine Ou
Production Manager: Alix Nicholaeff
Production Assistant: Sylvester Vang

ILLUSTRATOR CREDITS
Pages 9, 10, 12, 18, 35, 41, 74, 103, 108–109: Britt Wilson

IMAGE CREDITS
Page 6: © Mega Pixel / Shutterstock.com; Page 15: © farbled / Shutterstock.com;
Page 36: © koss13 / Shutterstock.com; Page 38: © Niki Crucillo / Shutterstock.com;
Page 44: © Joe Gough / Shutterstock.com; Page 50: © margouillat photo / Shutterstock.com;
Page 54: © Bernd Juergens / Shutterstock.com; Page 55: © Elena Shashkina / Shutterstock.com;
Page 58: © Aimee M Lee/ Shutterstock.com;
Page 93: © Anna Hoychuk / Shutterstock.com; Page 101: © arfo / Shutterstock.com

ROOTS of PEACE   REPLANTED PAPER

Insight Editions, in association with Roots of Peace, will plant two trees for each tree used in the manufacturing of this book. Roots of Peace is an internationally renowned humanitarian organization dedicated to eradicating land mines worldwide and converting war-torn lands into productive farms and wildlife habitats. Roots of Peace will plant two million fruit and nut trees in Afghanistan and provide farmers there with the skills and support necessary for sustainable land use.

Manufactured in China by Insight Editions

10 9 8 7 6 5 4

DATE DUE

Minerva Campbell

FOUNDERS' ISLAND
PUBLIC LIBRARY